Title: We Do Not Welcome Our Ten-Year-Old Overlord

Author: Garth Nix

On-Sale Date: October 15, 2024

Format: Jacketed Hardcover

ISBN: 978-1-339-01220-9 || Price: $18.99 US

Ages: 9–12

Grades: 4–7

LOC Number: Available

Length: 240 pages

Trim: 5-1/2 x 8-1/4 inches

Classification: Juvenile Fiction:

Science Fiction; Alien Contact / Historical; United States;

20th Century / Family; Siblings / Humorous Stories

---------------- *Additional Formats Available* --------------

Ebook ISBN: 978-1-546-10972-3

Scholastic Press
An Imprint of Scholastic Inc.
557 Broadway, New York, NY 10012
For information, contact us at:
tradepublicity@scholastic.com

WE DO NOT WELCOME
OUR

TEN-YEAR-OLD OVERLORD

WE DO NOT WELCOME OUR TEN-YEAR-OLD OVERLORD

GARTH NIX

SCHOLASTIC PRESS / NEW YORK

Copyright © 2024 by Garth Nix

All rights reserved. Published by Scholastic Press, an imprint of Scholastic Inc.,
Publishers since 1920. SCHOLASTIC, SCHOLASTIC PRESS, and associated logos are
trademarks and/or registered trademarks of Scholastic Inc.

The publisher does not have any control over and does not assume any responsibility
for author or third-party websites or their content.

No part of this publication may be reproduced, stored in a retrieval system, or
transmitted in any form or by any means, electronic, mechanical, photocopying,
recording, or otherwise, without written permission of the publisher. For information
regarding permission, write to Scholastic Inc., Attention: Permissions Department,
557 Broadway, New York, NY 10012.

This book is a work of fiction. Names, characters, places, and incidents are either the
product of the author's imagination or are used fictitiously, and any resemblance to
actual persons, living or dead, business establishments, events, or locales is entirely
coincidental.

Library of Congress Cataloging-in-Publication Data available

ISBN 978-1-339-01220-9

10 9 8 7 6 5 4 3 2 1   24 25 26 27 28

Printed in U.S.A.   66

First edition, October 2024

Book design by Maeve Norton

To the memory of my brother
Jonathan Nix
1966–2023
A creative genius in many fields, and one of the best
and kindest people I have ever known.

This book is set in an alternate version of Canberra, Australia, in a 1975 that did not exist. I have taken liberties with everything, particularly geography, history, the natural environment, and the release date of Dungeons & Dragons supplements.

While this story is not set in the actual Canberra, it is inspired by the real place, and I acknowledge the Ngunnawal people as traditional custodians of that land and pay my respects to elders past, present, and emerging.

Though none of the characters are based on real people and the family situations and everything else are all completely invented for a better story, this book is dedicated to the players of the D&D campaign I ran from roughly 1976 to 1981: Grant Flitton (Altmoor) and Peter Howe (Flàdrif), who both sadly left this plane of existence far too early; John Ciempka (Borkum Scandinavic); and Phil Greaves (Philip Des Cheveaux).

CHAPTER ONE

Without warning, the sun went out. Only for a fraction of a second, but it was definitely gone. Or so claimed the one scientist who had been paying attention. It was 1975, and the computers monitoring the few solar telescopes that were watching were not very advanced, so it was presumed to be a programming glitch or something like that. All the other scientists said she was wrong.

But the scientist wasn't wrong. In that split second the sun *had* disappeared and come back again, and the world had changed, even if no one knew it. Reality had rippled and bent, and there was suddenly something new on the earth that had not been there before.

A small globe, golden and shining, appeared in the shallows of an artificial lake. For a few moments it lit up the water—until it rolled around and coated itself in mud, and the light was dimmed. It continued to roll on, into a patch of weed that wrapped around it, fronds trailing up like hair from a severed head.

It was a twelve-minute ride down to that lake from Kim

Basalt's home, an easy coast even on his heavy old bicycle and a breeze on Bennie Chance's new ten-speed. Their younger siblings, Eila and Madir, took longer, always following but never catching up.

Kim, whose full name was Chimera Xanthoparmelia Basalt, was twelve years old, as was his best friend Bennie, whose full name was Benjamina Ramella Chance. Their younger sisters were only ten years old, Eileithyia Indigofera Basalt and Madir Sofitela Chance. They had known each other all their lives, but each pair became friends in preschool because, for that time, they had unusual names.

The quartet rode down to the lake almost every evening, after dinner for Kim and Eila because their parents insisted on eating together early, and before dinner for Bennie and Madir, whose meals were generally late and unpredictable. First Kim would ride down from the experimental farm on the mountain (a hill really) where his family lived to Bennie's house, which was on the highest street of the suburb below the mountain, with Eila trailing behind. Bennie would be ready and ride out straight away, with Madir yelling out to Eila to wait for her as she put on her shoes or looked for her hair band or whatever.

The night the globe appeared was like any other night

for the kids, at first. Once they got to the lake, Kim and Bennie put their bikes down by the boat ramp and sat on the park bench by the pebble-strewn foreshore to chat and skip stones, while Eila and Madir lounged on the round-about in the playground behind, idly pushing it with their feet while they talked. The two groups were far enough apart that neither group could hear what the other duo was talking about, which was the way they all liked it.

For Kim, it was a break from having Eila always know more about almost everything than he did, and telling him about it. His sister never held back, no matter how many times he tried to tell her that people often didn't like being corrected. And by "people," he meant himself.

Eila liked hanging out with Madir, because Mad worshipped Eila and was always happy to listen to her talk about anything. Also, it was a break for Madir from her own older sibling, Bennie being an ever watchful presence. But as long as she could keep an eye on her sister, Bennie didn't need to listen to her. So the separation suited everyone.

"Dan Lovell's family got a color TV," said Bennie. Color television had only been introduced eighteen months before, years later than in most other countries. She picked up a stone and idly threw it across the water lapping near their feet. It skipped four times and sank. This was a poor result for her, as she was a champion stone-skipper and generally fantastic at throwing anything, bowling in cricket, or pitching in softball.

"Remember that American girl whose family visited last year?" continued Bennie.

"Yeah. Rose."

"She couldn't believe no one had a color TV yet," said Bennie. She laughed and threw another stone. It skipped six times. "She must have looked in everyone's house, everyone in fifth grade, anyway. Demented."

"She didn't come to visit us," said Kim.

"Yeah, well, obviously," said Bennie.

Kim nodded, acknowledging the point. His family didn't have even a black-and-white television, and were never going to get one. His parents were dedicated to what they called an "alternative lifestyle," which was why they took the job looking after the experimental farm. It had six long greenhouses, and besides the actual scientific crops, Kim reckoned a bit too much of the space was taken up with the family's vegetables.

He was always worried his parents would get fired, but the scientists from the university down the hill and the government research center farther west along the ridge didn't seem to mind. Possibly because they were regularly given baskets of tomatoes and beans and zucchinis and out of season flowers.

Eila, on the other hand, did not share his anxiety. Sometimes Kim felt like his parents and sister lived in a different world to the one he inhabited. They were all so certain about everything, in their different ways. He wished he had their single-mindedness sometimes, but try as he might, he couldn't stop worrying about things that might happen, or could happen, or were definitely going to happen.

"Wish I had a bow," said Bennie, skipping another stone. She mimed shooting an arrow up at the sky, which was beginning to darken, the sun already out of sight behind the mountain, though its reddish light still lingered. "Like Flàdrif."

Flàdrif was the name of Bennie's character in a new game called Dungeons & Dragons. Kim had found it browsing in the city's one tiny games store, which mostly sold jigsaw puzzles and chess sets. He was immediately drawn to the small white box with the picture of a wizard blowing up a bunch of little monsters (orcs or goblins, he figured out later, and not blowing them up but casting a fireball). He stood for an hour carefully but swiftly reading through the three booklets the box contained, with the patient shop owner, Mrs. Griffith, only reminding him to not bend the pages.

After that first read, Kim wasn't really sure how you played the game, and Mrs. Griffith didn't know either, because it had only been released the year before and none of her customers had ever played it. But Kim desperately wanted to try the game. He loved fantasy books, and had already read *The Lord of the Rings* twice.

This game seemed to promise you could make up your own stories of monsters and magic and kind of act them out. Kim and Bennie already did, pretending to be Egyptians in a wholly imaginary pyramid on the school oval, fighting mummies, or Vikings in a longboat sailing out to combat frost giants, when they got a turn in one of the school canoes, going up and down the river just before it entered the lake.

The Dungeons & Dragons box was $20.00, which was $19.80 more than Kim had in the whole world, and he was lucky to have twenty cents in the first place, since his parents didn't believe in pocket money. Or money in general, for that matter.

Fortunately Bennie had a lot more than twenty dollars saved, and when she heard about the game, she came with him to the shop, they read through the books together, and she bought the box.

"Are we going to play again this Sunday?" asked Bennie.

"Sure," said Kim. They'd played three times so far, on Sunday afternoons, but they were getting the hang of it, or thought they were. Bennie played the elf fighter Flàdrif, and their fellow sixth-grade friends Theo and Tamara were, respectively, Altmoor the human magic user and Hargrim the dwarf cleric.

Kim was the Dungeon Master, which meant that he was the one who made up the basic outline of the story and described what was happening according to the players' decisions, the rules, and the roll of the dice.

He liked running the game, but he also wanted to play himself, and hoped he would one day. But they didn't know anyone else who played or had even heard of Dungeons & Dragons, and no one in the rest of the group wanted to run a game; they all liked playing too much.

Eila and Madir had expressed interest in playing when Kim was first talking about the game, but he told them it would only work for three players and a Dungeon Master. This was a straight-out lie. The real reason was because Kim thought his sister would argue with him all the time if she played. He wanted to do something Eila didn't know about. He even hid the rules so Eila couldn't read them.

"Can we play at your place again?" asked Kim. His parents didn't approve of any kind of war games, which is what they would think Dungeons & Dragons was, so he'd been careful not to tell them about it. They wouldn't even let Kim play Risk, which had been his and Bennie's favorite game before they discovered D&D.

Bennie shrugged, which meant it was no problem. Her parents were so busy with their own lives they seemed to Kim to barely notice their children, beyond attending to the bare necessities. They had never even attended a single parent-teacher night at school, which made all the other kids envious.

Not that Bennie saw it that way. She had tried to explain that the lack of parental attention was part of an actual problem, but Kim didn't understand. He could see only the advantages. Like being able to play D&D there and have sugar in his tea and not have parents giving him jobs to do all the time. Bennie's parents had big important jobs, and neither of them spent much time at home. They even had a cleaner come in, and a gardener, which no one else's parents did.

Bennie was just about to skip another stone, but she stopped as Eila suddenly walked in front of them and swiftly waded into the water. For a second both older kids gaped at her, before Kim sprang up and splashed in after his sister, with Bennie jumping across to restrain Madir as she tried to follow Eila into the lake. She always followed Eila in everything.

"Eila! What are you doing? Stop!" Kim called out.

But Eila didn't stop.

She never listened to her older brother, because Eila knew she was always right.

CHAPTER TWO

Eila stopped, but it wasn't because Kim was shouting at her. She suddenly knelt down in the water to look at something below the surface. Her brother grabbed her shoulder to pull her up, but she resisted.

He looked down as well and recoiled.

"What is that?" he asked. "Is that . . . a head?"

"Looks like it," whispered Bennie, coming up close. She had a tight grip on Madir, who was still trying to move up to Eila. "A cut-off head. Someone with long hair. A murderer must have thrown it in—"

"It isn't a cut-off head," snapped Eila. As so often, she used her "I told you so" voice, which Kim was always trying to get her to drop. Eila was super, super smart and nearly always right about facts, but telling people they were wrong often got her into trouble, particularly with older children. Kim and Bennie sometimes had to step in to protect her from bullies who didn't like being corrected by a know-it-all girl.

Kim peered into the murky water. "Yeah, the hair is lakeweed. It's an old cannonball or something like that. Or maybe just a stone?"

"*She* isn't a stone," corrected Eila. She shrugged Kim's hand off and leaned into the water to reach for the muddy ball, weed and all.

"Don't!" shouted Kim, but he was too late. Eila got both hands on whatever it was and lifted it out of the water, drawing it close to her chest. It was perfectly round, roughly the size of the globe in the school library, and pinpoints of light began to shine through where the mud was rubbing off.

Kim reached out to wrestle the globe away, and Bennie let go of Madir to help him. But as soon as they touched the muddy ball, they froze. Brilliant light shone *through* their fingers, showing their bones like shadows beneath the skin. They could not let go, nor move any other muscle.

Kim felt a sudden, sharp pain behind both ears, as if someone had stuck needles in either side of his head. But he couldn't even flinch, and a terror rose up inside him, accompanied by a horrible sensation that *something* was entering his brain. Incredibly thin fingers or tendrils squirming into his mind, feeling their way inside. At the same time he heard a voice, a voice he knew was not transmitted via sound through the air, but coming down those tendrils, straight into his head.

Let me in, said the voice. *Let me in. I am a friend. I can help you.*

No no heck no! thought Kim.

He exerted all his willpower, focusing his entire mind on getting free. His hands came off the globe as if wrenched away from some supersticky glue. Bennie was still holding on, blood trickling from the corner of her mouth where she had bit her lip, her eyes bulging as if she was trying to resist some incredible weight that was about to pull her underwater.

Kim grabbed his friend's wrists and pulled. For a moment he felt those needles again, trying to get into his brain, and then he and Bennie fell away together, into the lake, crashing below the surface. The cold, muddy water was a relief, the shock of it purging the sensation of those terrible tendrils probing inside their brains.

They came spluttering up, holding on to each other, to see Eila had walked back to shore, clutching the globe. Madir was holding Eila's elbow but not touching the globe itself. With a growing horror, Kim realized he'd managed to save his best friend . . . but not his sister.

Kim tried to talk but could only cough up water. He and Bennie waded ashore and shook themselves like dogs, sending droplets flying everywhere. Kim coughed a few more times and tried to talk again.

"Eila! Throw it away! It tried to get inside my head!"

For a split second he thought she might listen to him, possibly for the first time in her life.

But instead of dropping the globe onto the ground, Eila held it tighter.

"That is simply a more effective mode of communication," said Eila. She did not look at Kim. She was concentrating on smearing the mud more evenly across the globe, hiding those points of internal light. "It was rude of you to refuse."

"I don't think so," urged Kim. "Please, Eila! Throw it back!"

"*She* is a person," pronounced Eila.

"I'll tell Dad," said Kim. "And Mum!"

"No, you won't," said Eila, unperturbed. "Or I'll tell them about your Dungeons and Dragons game. And the war game you play with the Airfix soldiers. And your secret books."

Kim's secret books were simply novels. His parents only allowed nonfiction in the house, and only certain kinds at that. He kept his small personal store of books and those he'd borrowed from the school and city libraries inside the huge hollowed-out gum tree, which had been lazily used to anchor the perimeter fence, like a giant post on the northwest corner of the experimental farm.

"I'll tell *my* parents," snapped Bennie. "Madir, get away from it!"

"Eila says it's perfectly safe," Madir replied worshipfully, gripping Eila's elbow more tightly than ever. "It's our secret."

"You won't tell anyone either, Bennie," said Eila.

"Oh, won't I—"

"No, you won't, because your parents are too busy for you. They always are, aren't they?"

"That's not true," protested Bennie, but her voice was weak.

"Go on, then," said Eila. "Tell them. I guess you'll have to make an appointment—"

She didn't have to say any more. Bennie made a sound that was half a sob and half a growl, but didn't speak.

"I don't care if our parents stop my games or take my books," Kim said. "I am going to tell them."

Eila finally looked up from the globe and stared at him.

"Why?" she asked, exasperated. "There's no need. It will only cause trouble, mainly for you. It isn't rational. She's a friend!"

"I'm telling," said Kim. He remembered the touch of the globe reaching inside his head, how it hadn't backed off, how he'd had to use every particle of willpower he had to make it go. That wasn't the action of a friend.

Kim wanted to grab the globe from Eila and throw it out as far as he could, out into the deep, deep water. He was bigger and stronger, and Bennie would help. But he was afraid. He'd only just managed to escape those cold tendrils reaching into his brain. He might not be able to escape again. And who knew what else the globe could do?

Eila suddenly swiveled to look at the western sky. There was still a tiny sliver of sun visible, but it dipped beneath the horizon as she watched. An afterglow remained.

A flake of mud fell off the globe, and its light shone through. But it was no longer bright and golden; it was a dark, subdued red.

"Oh," said Eila, but she was not speaking to Kim, Bennie, or Madir. "You can do that? Yes, that's a good idea."

She looked back at Kim, meeting her brother's troubled gaze with her own obstinate, certain eyes.

"What are you going to tell Mum and Dad, anyway?"

Kim pointed at the globe. But only for a moment, before he let his hand fall. He heard Bennie gasp beside him, and Madir let out a little cry of triumph.

"Are you going to tell them I found a basketball in the lake?"

Eila drew her fingers across the globe, scraping off mud.

The light faded under her hand to reveal orange stippled rubber decorated with thin black lines.

The globe had transformed itself into a basketball, like the old ones they had at school, worn and well used.

Harmless and ordinary.

CHAPTER THREE

It was three days since they had found the globe. Everything had been normal since then; nothing terrible had happened. But Kim couldn't stop thinking about it.

"What can we do?" he asked Bennie.

The two of them were sitting on their bikes on the higher bank of the stormwater drain that ran along the ridge about fifty yards above the experimental farm. Unlike the drains farther down in the city, which were concrete, this one was just a deep cut in the red earth. It was dry most of the time, as it was now, and crisscrossed with trails where kids rode their bikes down one side and up the other, often falling off along the way. At this particularly steep part of the drain, the track across was known as the Dipper.

"About what?" asked Bennie. She gestured at the earthen channel below them. "You going to go?"

"Eila. The globe thing," said Kim. "You felt it—it was trying to get into our minds!"

Bennie shrugged. It was characteristic of her to not be bothered by anything for long. She dealt with problems or learned to live with them. Kim was the one who couldn't stop thinking and going over possibilities, both good and bad.

"Eila seems okay with it," Bennie pointed out.

Kim shrugged unhappily. Eila had avoided him every time he tried to talk to her about the globe. But as Bennie said, apart from that, she seemed to be the same as ever. He winced, remembering the conversation at dinner the night before, when he'd got confused about the names of two plant species and his parents *and* Eila had corrected him.

"What if it's taken control of her?"

"You reckon anything could take control of Eila? More likely the other way around. There's nothing we can do, anyway."

"We could take it back to the lake and chuck it in," said Kim.

"Yeah? Do you know where Eila's got it? Do you want to touch it again?"

"Nuh. But we could use your prawn net to carry it. And there's not that many places she could hide it—"

"On the whole farm?" asked Bennie.

Kim couldn't answer that. He'd been thinking she would hide it in the house.

"I'll find it," he said.

"Okay, then."

With that, Bennie put her feet up on her pedals, pushed down hard, and launched her bike down the slope, speeding across the slightly muddy bottom of the drain to roar triumphantly up the other side, sliding to a halt on the lower embankment, assisted by both brakes, and putting her feet down either side to send up a cloud of dust and gravel.

"Come on!" she called.

Kim sighed, got up properly on his heavy old bike and started down, much more slowly and wobbly than Bennie. He hit the bottom, skidded in the mud and crashed into the other side instead of riding up. He fell off sideways and the bike slid down.

"Ow!" said Kim, mostly from habit. His knees and left elbow were scraped, beads of blood showing, but otherwise he was unhurt.

"You didn't push off," said Bennie critically. "You want a go on my bike?"

Kim shook his head. "Nah, thanks. I've got to get back and weed the carrots, anyway. You want to help?"

"Nope," said Bennie. "Remember last time, I pulled up more carrots than weeds? I don't know how you can tell the difference. Your parents were a bit cross."

"Practice," said Kim, rather grimly. He spent a lot of time weeding.

"Everything still okay for the game tomorrow?"

"Yep," said Kim. "I've got a couple of things left to do, but I'm pretty much ready."

Because Eila had been avoiding him and he couldn't pin her down to ask her questions, Kim had distracted himself by working on the D&D adventure for Sunday, designing a dungeon beneath a tavern, the composition of bands of wandering monsters, a powerful wizard who might be an enemy or a friend, depending . . .

He already knew half of or more of what he'd prepared wouldn't be used, the players would do things he hadn't even thought of, go off in directions he couldn't anticipate, but it was still a lot of fun to work out. Even better, his parents thought he was doing extra homework and had let him off some of his regular chores.

But not the carrot weeding. And after that he had to chip mortar off used bricks from a giant pile, all that was left of some old building on the farm, demolished long before the Basalt family got there. His mother would reuse the bricks to make garden paths. Kim estimated there were three thousand bricks, and it took him a couple of minutes to chip the mortar off each one with a serrated-head hammer, except occasionally some bricks would be really difficult and take four or five minutes.

So there was probably 9,000 minutes of work to be done, which was 150 hours. At a minimum of one hour a week, as his mother had instructed, it would take him . . . roughly forever.

But that was the way things were in the Basalt family. Everyone worked. School had priority for Kim and Eila, but there were a lot of jobs that came after that, with having fun way down the list of priorities.

The Basalt family. His parents had chosen the name. Kim wasn't sure what his parents' original surnames had been, though he suspected his mother's was Jones because that was his grandmother's surname. Grannie Jones was the only relative he'd ever met, but she lived a long way away, so he'd only seen her three times in his whole life so far.

His parents said they chose Basalt because it was a rock they liked, and a strong name. Their children's middle names were also meaningful, at least to botanists. *Xanthoparmelia* was the scientific name for a family of lichen, his father's favorite, just as Eila's middle name was also a plant family, in this case their mother's choice: *Indigofera*.

It was clever, Kim thought, but a real pain when it came

to putting his name on forms for school or whatever, because no one ever believed him. He'd spent a long fifteen minutes once trying to make a deputy principal understand he wasn't joking about his middle name, after a struggle over him being really "Chimera" and not "Kim" and how his proper name was pronounced "kim-era."

Admittedly, he had a massively bloody nose at the time and a puffed-up lip, the result of running too fast, slipping on an icy corner of the playground and colliding with the side of the school. He'd been racing Bennie, who of course had won. They'd both ended up in front of the deputy because they'd been out of bounds *and* racing.

Now he and Bennie walked their bikes from the storm-water drain down to the farm entrance. The whole place was surrounded by high security fencing and huge warning signs that read GOVERNMENT PROPERTY. EXPERIMENTAL FARM. KEEP OUT, but in fact the gates were very rarely closed.

"You want to go down to the lake later?" asked Bennie. Usually this wouldn't be a question; Kim would simply ride down to Bennie's place and off they'd go. But they hadn't been back since finding the globe, and though they hadn't talked about it, both were uncomfortable about going down there again.

"Nah," said Kim. "I'll do some more work, get ready for the game."

"Okay, see you tomorrow. About eleven, right?"

Bennie rode away, very fast, head down. Kim went on through the gates and put his bike away in the huge shed that served as a garage for the visiting scientists. The Basalts didn't have a car—they all had bikes like Kim's, ancient and heavy, old post office bicycles that Kim's father had bought as a job lot. There were eight of them in the shed, in various states of repair.

Kim went straight to greenhouse three. He hesitated when he saw Eila was already there, weeding one of the long beds of carrots. The heavy steel-and-glass door squealed as he opened it. That was another job he was supposed to do: oil all the doors.

"Six minutes and I'm done," said Eila. She didn't have a watch to look at, but Kim didn't doubt her. She had an uncanny sense of time, and would have spent the whole hour required. Eila always did all the chores their parents insisted on exactly. Never more, never less. "You can finish this row."

"Okay," Kim said, bending down farther along the row to start. It was incredible how many weeds managed to grow in the week since the last weeding, and how many of them resembled carrot plants. Even with all his practice over the years, he had to pay attention.

After a few minutes, he asked as casually as he could, "What's going on with that globe thing you found?"

Eila stopped weeding and looked at him. She had on her long-suffering expression, which meant she was doing her best to put up with the relative lack of intelligence of her brother.

"*She* is a person, not a 'globe thing,'" said Eila. "Her name is Aster. At least, that is the closest spoken word that suits. You know, from the Greek, for 'star.'"

Kim nodded as if he did know. Eila could read and write Latin and Greek, and French, German, Italian, and Spanish. She couldn't speak them well, because she'd taught herself from books and had mostly never heard how to pronounce the words properly. She had books for other languages too, Japanese and Chinese and Russian, but Kim didn't know how far along she was with those. Eila had once talked a lot about what she was learning, but not so much the last year or two, partly because Kim had advised her not to, since it annoyed the other kids and some of the teachers.

He still wasn't sure if that had been good advice, and whether he'd done it for her sake or his own. Having a too-smart little sister had often caused him trouble with older, bigger children. He wondered if he should have been braver about standing up for her, instead of trying to get her to keep more in the background.

"So where is Aster from?" asked Kim, accidentally pulling out a carrot because he was distracted. He sighed and replanted it, though that probably wouldn't work. "And what is she?"

"She is a person, like I said," replied Eila. "And she doesn't know where's she from. She's kind of . . . lost."

"Lost?"

For the first time Eila looked uncertain.

"Taken a wrong turn? Mislaid? It's kind of hard to explain in our words."

"So what does she want? Why is she here?"

"She wants to learn. I'm helping her. The more she understands about us and our world, the better."

"Why?"

"So she can help, of course." Eila straightened up from the carrot row and stretched. "Help us."

"Help us how?" asked Kim. "What can she do?"

"She has to learn first," said Eila evasively. She stood up and brushed the earth off her hands. "Don't worry. She listens to me. I'll tell her what she can do to help us, when the time comes."

She walked away, ignoring Kim as he struggled to work out what to say. She was out of the greenhouse before he could put together the words he wanted. He said them anyway, even if was only to the carrots and himself.

"Eila, I'm not sure that's a good idea. I know you're super smart. Everyone knows that. But you're only ten, and let's face it, sometimes you're too smart for your own good—and everybody else's."

CHAPTER FOUR

Everyone went to bed early in the Basalt household. Or at least they were supposed to. Kim's parents didn't approve of using more electricity than was strictly necessary and wouldn't let him have the light on in his bedroom after nine o'clock. He got around that by using a bedside lamp Bennie had given him, and reading inside the ancient wardrobe that took up a good third of his room. Luckily there was an outlet in the wall behind it, so all he had to do was cut a hole in the back of the wardrobe for the electric cord and rearrange some of his clothes.

It was all a bit uncomfortable and claustrophobic, and the metal shade of the lamp got hot enough to burn him if he wasn't careful . . . but at least he could read. He knew he was safe from discovery by his parents, because they went to bed as soon as the lights were off. They got up at dawn and worked on the farm all day, so they were always tired.

He'd just finished reading chapter five of *A Wizard of Earthsea* and very reluctantly decided not to start chapter six. He'd turned off the light and was creeping out of the wardrobe when he heard something. At first he thought it was one of the possums that sometimes got into the ceiling and thumped around, before he realized it was the sound of a door being softly closed, followed by muffled footsteps going past his room.

Kim recognized the flapping of the loose left sole on Eila's favorite slippers. This was strange because Eila didn't sneak around at night. Or at least she never had before, as far as he knew. He opened his bedroom door as quietly as possible, peering out just in time to see the back door snick shut.

Quickly, he raced through the kitchen and looked out the window. The moon was up though it was only a sliver, but the sky was clear and the stars quite bright. He could just make out someone crossing the back lawn.

It was Eila, and she was carrying the globe. Or *Aster*, as she wanted to call it. He couldn't tell if Aster was still disguised as a basketball, but she wasn't glowing like she had been when he'd first seen her under the waters of the lake.

He slipped out the back door and followed, not bothering to go back for his shoes. Which was a mistake, he knew, as soon as he left the lawn and trod on a sharp stone. He had to stop and feel for an injury, but though it hurt a lot, it hadn't broken the skin.

In those few brief moments, he lost Eila. When he looked

around again, he couldn't see her anywhere close in the darkness. He stood listening for a minute, but that didn't help either. He heard a possum on the roof, and something small scurrying about on the fringe of the lawn, probably a bandicoot. But no soft footsteps.

He was about to give up and go back in when he caught a faint glimpse of light in the corner of his eye. Not from the streetlights down the hill, or the big perimeter lights of the research center a good five hundred yards away, familiarly twinkling through the dense trees. This was closer. Near the big tree at the corner of the fence, where he kept his books.

Kim turned toward the light and started walking slowly, taking care where he put his feet. He knew the path here well, between the smaller trees that had spread past the fence, thick bunches of eucalypt leaves hanging down overhead blocking the starlit sky.

The light had to be coming from the globe. It flickered now, very rapidly. Kim crept closer, squinting. Eila was holding the globe over her head and slightly forward, to illuminate the ground ahead of her.

Lighting up the big ant nest, Kim realized. A mound of red earth that came up past Eila's waist was the visible sign of the massive ant nest that lay beneath, probably extending for a long way in all directions. The ants were the red, biting kind, but they were no trouble as long as you didn't stand on or near the nest.

Like Eila was doing right now.

Kim surged forward, trod on a stick, and hopped the rest of the way, rubbing his big toe, feeling blood. He stopped a few feet short of his sister. He didn't want to get bitten. He had a few times, by one ant, and it really hurt. People often ended up in the hospital for weeks if they got stung by a lot of ants at once.

"Eila! Get away from the nest! You know the ants will bite."

"No they won't," said Eila. She didn't show her emotions, and as always Kim found it was hard to know what she was thinking, but she certainly wasn't afraid. "Aster is studying them."

Kim stopped, inspected his bleeding toe, and looked down. The ants were swarming out of the nest. Hundreds if not thousands of them came like a wave toward Eila's feet, and then, again like a wave, ebbed back, none reaching her. More and more ants came behind, but they also would not or could not get closer. As soon as they reached the circle of swiftly flickering light from the globe Eila held high, they turned around, fell back, or diverted to the sides, away from the light, into the darkness.

The light bothered Kim. It felt like a milder, less intrusive version of those tendrils that had tried to get into his head. He half shut his eyes, leaned closer without taking another step, and pulled at Eila's elbow. She shrugged him off.

"Don't! Aster needs more time."

"To do what?" asked Kim. He had to let go of Eila to keep his balance, and took two steps back. He felt a bit better out of the circle of light.

"I told you. She's studying the ants. Looking at how they're made, how they communicate, how their bodies work."

"Why?"

"Knowledge," said Eila. "Information. Aster wants to know how this world works, from the simplest life to the most complex."

"Why now? Why at night?" asked Kim. "You should be in bed asleep."

"So should you," said Eila, not answering his question.

"Come on, Eila!"

"I'm helping my friend learn something," snapped Eila. "Can't you understand that?"

Kim didn't know how to answer. He was frightened by the globe, by Aster. That flickering light, and the ants all turning away, as if being commanded to go back . . .

The light suddenly stopped flickering, and slowly dimmed. Eila lowered the globe. It briefly continued to glow faintly, but within seconds it was a dull, old basketball again.

"Aster's learned enough for now, anyway," Eila said. Then she walked away, back to the house.

Kim followed. He watched Eila carefully, noting that she took the globe into her bedroom. So it wouldn't be that hard to find. Whether Bennie helped him or not, he decided he would borrow her prawning net tomorrow, use it to lift the globe and take it down to the lake, wade in, and throw it into the deepest possible water.

After liberally daubing his cut toe with Dettol, Kim went to bed. But despite being tired, he couldn't sleep for quite a while. Every time he shut his eyes he saw the swift flicker of the globe's light, the swarming ants turning back, falling over themselves, and the fascinated expression on his sister's face.

CHAPTER FIVE

The morning did not begin well. Kim slept in and had to be woken by his mother, who did not appreciate it. Sunday was not a day of rest for the Basalt family. Kim's parents didn't believe in religion, or organized religion, anyway. There was always work to be done, in the greenhouses and plant beds.

After gulping down his lukewarm porridge (the Basalts alternated between cold granola and hot porridge, never anything else), Kim washed everyone's dishes and then went to help his father for an hour, shifting a hundred plants in small pots out of greenhouse six into the general nursery area. The pots had to be organized exactly as they'd been in the greenhouse, with all labels visible, or the experiment they were part of would be ruined.

Back at the house, Kim transferred the library copy of *A Wizard of Earthsea* from the pocket of his winter parka to the small of his back, tucking it in to his shorts so it wouldn't fall out. Then he put a tracksuit top on over his T-shirt to hide the book, even though it was early summer now and the days were warming up rapidly. In another month, two layers would look very weird and he'd have to think of some other way to smuggle the books in and out of the house from his hiding place. The other option was to give up secretly reading at night —and he wasn't going to do that.

Kim went out the front door of the house and slinked along the fence to the big tree at the corner. After checking he wasn't being observed, he got the old toolbox out of the decaying knot hole in the huge trunk, opened it, and slipped the book in with the others. Then he put the box back and covered it with strips of fallen bark.

Along the way home he stopped near the ant nest. It was busy as ever, with ants crawling in and out of various holes, lines of them transporting food and bits of leaves and all their other usual business.

But that wasn't why he'd stopped.

The spot where Eila had stood, where she had held the globe up, was surrounded by dead ants. Thousands of them, a thick carpet of carcasses, arrayed in a half circle about six feet in diameter. All the ants that had swarmed out to attack the intrusive human and had been turned back by Aster. They hadn't got very far before they died.

It was rare to see a dead ant at all, at least for very long. Ant corpses were always picked up by live ants and taken back to the nest.

But not these ones.

Kim watched for several minutes. The live ants from the nest were avoiding their dead this time. Every now and then, one would come close, then suddenly recoil and hurry back where it came from.

It was as if the dead ants were poison.

"That's it," whispered Kim to himself. He spoke aloud because it made him feel braver when he was not feeling brave at all. Quite the reverse. "That's it. I'm getting the net from Bennie *right now*, and I'm going to take the globe to the lake and throw it as far as I can throw it."

Maybe I can even get one of the school canoes and take the globe way out, he thought as he hurried to the front gate. Sometimes the PE teachers forgot to lock the padlock or loop the chain through all the canoes. Or perhaps he could "borrow" the yacht club dinghy, though it was Sunday, so there'd be bound to be lots of people around on their boats . . .

"Kim! There you are!"

Kim flinched as if he'd been shot in the chest with an arrow. For a moment he considered dropping and playing dead, but his mother wouldn't understand; she'd just get cross with him again.

He turned to face her, already knowing he wouldn't like

what he was going to hear next. His mother was carrying a cardboard box full of vegetables. That meant she wanted it taken somewhere. Probably to one of the scientists, who mostly lived nearby. But there was one potential delivery that was far, far more difficult—

"I need you to take this up to Mrs. Benison," said Marie Basalt. She'd chosen her first name too, after Marie Curie. Kim knew she had originally been called Peggy, because he'd heard an old friend of the family call her that, and his father "Gary," even though he was called Darwin now, after Charles Darwin. Kim thought he should have gone with Charles, but Darwin Basalt he was.

Mrs. Benison lived in the old homestead that was the sole house on the mountain proper, only fifty yards below the summit. It was supposed to be demolished soon. The existing television mast on top, which was a very basic hundred-foot-high open-framework tower held up with steel guy-ropes, was going to be replaced with a space-age tower six times as tall. The new tower was going to have a viewing platform and even a revolving restaurant. To cater for all the tourists who would come to this new attraction, a parking lot was planned for the shelf where Mrs. Benison's house had been built, the only flat area below the peak.

Construction of the tower kept being delayed. Bennie

had said it was because they were waiting for Mrs. Benison to die, since she had to be a hundred years old or something like that. Once she was gone, there would be no problem knocking her house down.

It would take forty-five minutes for Kim to walk up to Mrs. Benison's via the twisting road. It was a shorter distance if he went straight up through the bush, but much harder going, so that would take just as long, if not longer, and he'd arrive all scratched from low branches and spiky shrubs and would quite likely drop the box on the way and bruise the contents.

"Oh, Mum!" he said. "Can't one of the scientists take it up in their car?"

"Not today. You take it, please. It will be good exercise."

Kim sighed, walked over, and took the box. It held three small but crisp lettuces and a scattering of tomatoes, all greenhouse grown, and a jar of his mother's homemade strawberry jam. There had been a marvelous crop of strawberries the year before and Marie had made a lot of jam, but it was not really sweet, as she hadn't used enough sugar. Kim had looked up jam making later in the school library and figured she'd used less than a third of what was usual. It was more like a strawberry relish than a jam. His parents and Eila ate it, but Kim avoided it wherever possible. At least a jar going to Mrs. Benison meant one less at home.

"Give Mrs. Benison my respects and ask her if she needs any assistance with anything," said Marie. "And don't take any money if she offers you some. This is neighborly helping out."

"She lives half a mile away, all uphill," protested Kim. "Can't we help someone closer?"

"Mrs. Benison needs our help," said Marie. "Our closer neighbors do not. Off you go."

Kim nodded glumly, and started on his way. For a moment, he wondered what would happen if one of his parents found all the dead ants. If they asked him for an explanation, what could he possibly say? They'd never believe the truth. He could barely believe it himself.

To get to Mrs. Benison's, Kim had to go downhill first, to join the main street and follow it past the government laboratory to the mountain road. At least it was still early enough that he could get back in good time for the Dungeons & Dragons game, he figured as he trudged along.

And thankfully it wasn't hot. It had been sunny the day before, but it was cloudy now, and cooler. Even so, while the box wasn't exactly heavy, it was awkward and he knew it would certainly feel much heavier as he started to climb up, and he'd soon be sweaty and tired.

He was two-thirds of the way up the mountain when he had to stop, put the box down, and rest. Unlike the streets below, there was no footpath here, only a kind of eroded drain that doubled as a dirt track for walkers, on the edge of the single lane of the mountain road.

Kim had just put the box down, intending to sit next to it, when he heard a car engine roar up above, the squeal of tires losing grip, and a sound like hail that he knew was from spinning wheels scattering gravel.

He jumped up, grabbed the box, and stumbled three or four steps down the slope, trying to get clear of the road without tumbling down the mountainside.

Thirty seconds later, a white Ford sedan rushed past, too fast, its right-hand wheels off the road and in the dirt. Kim was sprayed with gravel, turning aside just in time so it impacted his back rather than his face.

The car didn't stop. Kim turned around in time to catch a glimpse of its rear license plate, which started with a red letter Z, indicating it was a government vehicle.

Shaking slightly from the near miss, Kim climbed back onto the road. He looked in the top of the box. The vegetables now had a coating of dust, but were otherwise all right; they hadn't been hit by anything big. He was okay too, despite being peppered with gravel.

He didn't stop to brush himself down. He didn't want to stay on the narrow, steep road any longer. The sooner he delivered the box, the better. Then he'd go home straight down the mountain, through the bush, avoiding the road altogether.

And speeding government cars. Which was weird, particularly on a Sunday.

What did someone from the government want with Mrs. Benison?

CHAPTER SIX

Kim was relieved a few minutes later when he came to where the road forked, one branch going up another fifty yards or so to the television mast on the summit, and the other slightly down toward the flat area where Mrs. Benison's house stood. It was an old colonial house, with a veranda all the way around and a corrugated iron roof that was painted a dull red, almost brown. It always looked the same, but this time Kim noticed there were lots of new bright yellow poles stuck in the ground around the house, and lines of yellow paint had been sprayed on the lawn.

Mrs. Benison was outside, on the veranda, looking up at the cloudy sky, shielding her eyes with her hand. After a moment or two, she noticed Kim and slowly brought her shielding hand down in a wave. He couldn't wave back since he was holding the box, but he nodded his head and smiled.

"Hello, Kim," said Mrs. Benison with a smile as Kim walked up to the front steps. She was white-haired, dark-skinned, and quite stooped. She moved very slowly, but she was always cheerful and her deep brown eyes were still sharp and watchful. "I hope my granddaughter didn't run you off the road. She always drives too fast. She's a police officer, you know. Always thinks she's about to be chasing someone."

"That was your granddaughter?" asked Kim. "I heard her car coming and got out of the way."

"Yes, Sheree is another one keen for me to leave this house," said Mrs. Benison. "Though at least it's because she wants me to live with her, not simply to knock the place down so they can start on their tower. Would you like a cup of tea?"

"Uh, no thanks. I have to get back. Mum sent me up with some veggies. Where should I put them?"

"Oh, the kitchen table, please." Mrs. Benison waved him toward the front door, which was open.

She followed him inside. Kim hadn't been in other parts of the house, but he knew the way to the kitchen. He had brought fruit, vegetables, and flowers to the old lady several times before, taking over from his parents when he turned eleven and was allowed to go on his own.

He always liked visiting, because the house was a kind of time capsule. Everything in it was from the 1920s or 1930s, from the faded Turkish carpet in the hallway to the furniture. The kitchen was all tiled like a bathroom, and the stove and the refrigerator were both enormous, eggshell-blue electric appliances that had to be decades old but still worked perfectly. Kim particularly liked the refrigerator because it looked like a robot, the cooling unit separate on top so it looked like it had a head.

Unfortunately, seeing the robotic refrigerator made him think of the globe and how he'd initially thought it looked like a cut-off head. He shivered as he put the box down on the red Laminex-topped kitchen table.

"A shiver!" exclaimed Mrs. Benison. "After all the hard work of coming up the hill? Are you all right, Kim?"

She always called the mountain a hill. Apparently it had only been called a mountain the last fifty years, in an attempt to make it sound more important.

"I'm fine, thanks." Kim looked at Mrs. Benison for a moment, into her wise, old eyes, and briefly wondered if he could tell her about the globe. Maybe she could advise him. But he dismissed the thought. No adult would believe him, particularly if they only saw a basketball. Besides, he already knew what he needed to do. He was going to get the net from Bennie and after D&D, take the globe back to the lake and chuck it in. Then everything would be okay.

"Goose walking on your grave, perhaps," said

Mrs. Benison. When Kim looked blank, she added, "It's just a saying. When you shiver for no reason."

She took the kettle from the stove and went to fill it up at the sink. Unlike everyone else Kim knew, she didn't use an electric kettle, but an old copper one with a silver whistle, that went on the stove. "You sure you don't want a cup of tea? Or a glass of water?"

"No, I have to get back," said Kim. "Straight down, through the bush."

"Much faster, for the young and swift," said Mrs. Benison. She flipped the tap and let the kettle fill. As she leaned back, Kim saw her grimace, pain scrunching up her face for a second or two.

"Are you all right, Mrs. B?" he asked.

"I'm very old and I have at least three medical problems the doctors can point to, but I'm all right," said Mrs. Benison. She smiled again. "I'm ninety-six, Kim. Very few people live to such an age. If it wasn't for this new tower business, I wouldn't have a care in the world. Particularly not with kind people like you and your family looking after me."

Kim looked down, embarrassed. He never even thought about Mrs. Benison, except when his mum or dad asked him to take a box up to her. He didn't feel he really deserved her gratitude.

"I hope you get to stay here as long as you want," he said. He hesitated, then added, "I saw the poles and the markings and everything, outside."

"Oh yes," said Mrs. Benison with a sigh. "The surveyors have been at work. A gentle encouragement for me to get on with leaving. Or dying, I suppose. My husband couldn't cope with it at all." She took the full kettle over to the stove and set it on the hot plate. "He could be an angry man, and he got so angry at the government taking his land, first for the city and the lake and then for the tower, that he had a heart attack and died. That's almost five years ago now. Of course, he was already very old, like me."

Kim had a vague memory of Mr. Benison. A tall man who walked with a stick and had pale skin that was often sunburned red.

"I made him angrier because I told him it was not unjust, given that his family had stolen the land from the original people, anyway," Mrs. Benison continued, looking down at the bright kettle and not at the boy. "His family might have farmed the valley below for a hundred years, but the indigenous people were here for tens of thousands of years before that. I don't suppose you know any of that history. Not taught in school, is it?"

Kim shook his head.

"It should be," said Mrs. Benison firmly. "I hope it will be, one day."

Kim nodded.

Mrs. Benison smiled at him. Kim nodded again, and shifted nervously on the spot, standing on one foot then the other. He didn't know what to say.

"Thank you again for the vegetables," said Mrs. Benison. "I hope I will see you again soon."

"Me too," said Kim. He understood he could go now without being rude. He edged out the door, but the old lady followed him to the veranda.

"Be careful, Kim," she said as he walked away. There was a bit of track leading from the lawn, probably made by kangaroos coming up to nibble the well-watered grass. "Something odd is going on. The air is too still, and that cloud . . ."

Kim stopped and looked up. He hadn't really noticed before, apart from being glad it wasn't sunny and hot when he was coming up the mountain. There was a thin, perfectly circular layer of cloud directly above them, covering the city. But beyond this circle the sky was quite blue.

"That cloud has been growing," said Mrs. Benison with a frown. "Since yesterday. It should have been broken up by the wind, or moved on. But it sits there, spreading farther by the hour. If it was high summer and a bushfire burning, I would think it was smoke. But it is not fire season yet, I can smell no smoke, and there have been no warnings on the radio. I suppose there is some scientific explanation. But I do not like it."

"Neither do I," said Kim. The cloud's circular shape reminded him all too much of the globe. He felt sure it was something to do with Aster. The sooner he got rid of her, the better.

He waved and started down the kangaroo track. He heard the kettle begin to whistle inside the house as he left, growing sharper and more shrill, as if it was a warning of things to come.

CHAPTER SEVEN

Kim was almost home, above the Dipper drain, when he saw Eila. She was on the lower embankment, watching a mob of kangaroos on the grassy slope below. She wasn't carrying the globe. She was just standing there. Watching.

There were usually quite a few gray kangaroos around the lower part of the mountain; they even ventured into the city in particularly dry times, to eat well-watered lawn grass and the like, and were far less nervous of humans than was usual.

As far as Kim knew, Eila had never been interested in kangaroos. At least he'd never seen her pay them any particular attention. She was watching them carefully now, particularly one kangaroo on the edge of the mob. Kim dropped down into a crouch and kept still, watching Eila watch the kangaroos.

Finally, Eila moved, walking down. The kangaroos reacted, bounding away for several hops before stopping to look back at her, ears twitching.

Except for the one Eila had been looking at in particular.

There was something wrong with it; it didn't so much as hop as lurch away, barely keeping upright. Kim frowned. It had probably been hit by a car, crossing a road, or maybe got tangled up in a fence. It would almost certainly die.

Why was Eila particularly interested in an injured kangaroo?

"Eila!" shouted Kim as he ran down to her. The kangaroos leaped away at his shout, retreating up the hillside. Even the hurt one got away.

His sister stopped and looked back. Her expression was as calm and enigmatic as ever.

"Yes?"

"Why were you watching that sick kangaroo?"

"She isn't sick," replied Eila. "She has injured the tendons in her legs and possibly her tail."

"You didn't answer my question. Why were you watching her?"

"To ascertain her injuries. She was hit by a car, I think. Not a truck or anything larger. Aster will be interested."

"Why didn't you bring her, then?"

Eila didn't answer immediately. For a moment, Kim thought she might be about to lie to him and was making something up. But Eila didn't lie.

"Aster likes nighttime better."

"What?"

Eila started walking downhill again.

"Why doesn't Aster like the sun?" Kim shouted after her. "Why can't she come out in the light?"

Eila didn't answer.

Kim followed her home, wanting to ask more questions, but it was already ten forty-five by the kitchen clock, so he had barely enough time to gather up his Dungeons & Dragons materials (disguised within a couple of textbooks in his schoolbag) and head down to Bennie's. He was nearly given another job by his dad but saw him in time to duck around the back of greenhouse three and scuttle out of the farm—not through the main gate but via one of the holes in the perimeter fence on the southern side.

Bennie, Theo, and Tamara were waiting outside Bennie's house. Madir was sitting on the steps, reading a book.

Kim looked up and saw the menacingly circular cloud above them but decided not to say anything. He felt like something terrible was beginning, building up, heading toward disaster. But it was only a feeling, nothing he could properly explain. Maybe the cloud was only a cloud. It wasn't as if it was a giant monster he could point at and scream out a warning.

"Hey," said Bennie, checking her watch. She had a new

Texas Instruments digital watch that glowed in the dark; her mother had brought it back from one of her many business trips to the United States. "You're almost late."

"Why're you out here?" asked Kim.

"We have to play in the garage," Bennie replied. "We don't want to wake up Mum and Dad. Mum only flew in from New York last night, and Dad was at the office for some crisis; he didn't get home until five this morning. Better they sleep."

Madir, though apparently intent on her book, nodded deeply in agreement.

"Sure," Kim said. Though he'd known Bennie for years, he could count the number of times he'd met her parents on one hand. They were always busy with their work. Up until Bennie turned twelve, she and Madir had been looked after by various nannies. But they had often changed; none lasted even a year. Bennie said that this was because her parents set impossible standards for everyone but themselves.

Kim dropped his bike on the lawn and followed Bennie away from the house.

Bennie's garage was huge, a triple-car space, but her parents never put their cars in there. It had an old kitchen sink in one corner with only cold water, a toilet out the back, and in the middle a Ping-Pong table was permanently set up. There was also an old lounge, two coffee tables, several mismatched chairs, a refrigerator that was usually empty, and a useless dartboard.

It was useless because all the darts were really blunt and wouldn't stick in. This was probably just as well, as Bennie sometimes threw them at people. They wouldn't go through a shirt and she nearly always hit where she aimed, below the neck, but every now and then someone would get struck in a bare arm or hand.

It took a while for everyone to settle down, as it always did, but eventually Kim had handed out the character sheets, put down the map he'd drawn for the players (without a lot of the information on his own version) on the bigger coffee table, got the dice laid out next to the map, and stopped Bennie from throwing a dart at Tamara.

"Okay," he said. "When we finished last week, you'd just arrived outside the walls of the town of Shir, as the sun is setting. Shir is one of Mirraniel's major ports and there's lots of trade there. The docks are dangerous, because there are tons of thieves and drunken sailors and even out-of-work assassins keeping in practice."

"Let's go there, then," said Bennie.

"Let's not," countered Theo. "We've got a job, remember? We have to deliver this scroll to the town wizard."

"We're outside the walls?" asked Tamara. "Is there a gate?"

"You're on the road leading to the massive oak-and-black-steel gate, which is just beginning to shut for the night," said Kim. "Horns are being blown on the walls, alerting everyone—"

"Alerting them to what? I look around," said Bennie, "and ready my bow."

"Alerting everyone that the gate is being shut," said Kim.

"We'd better get inside," said Theo. "I run to the gate."

"Me too," chorused Tamara and Bennie.

"Luckily the gate is very heavy and slow to close," Kim told them. "There is still a gap. But there are two town guards standing in the gap, and many more on the walls above with crossbows. Uh, you know the usual toll to enter is a silver piece each."

"I could shoot them," said Bennie.

"No!" screamed Theo. "We'd get killed. I hold up a gold piece as we approach and wave it around."

"The gold coin catches the light of the setting sun; the glint from it catches the eyes of the guards," said Kim. "One of them at the gate grabs it from your hand as you run up, and they stand aside and let you pass. Make sure you cross off a gold piece, Theo."

"That reminds me," interrupted Tamara. "Did we get the treasure and the experience points from that band of goblins we fought at the end of last session, on the hill above the town?"

"Uh, no, you didn't. But I said I'd do it this week, didn't I? We'll get to that in a minute. You've got past the gate, which crashes shut. A troll comes out of the guardhouse—"

"I nock an arrow," snapped Bennie.

"Nock?" asked Tamara.

"When you get an arrow ready but don't pull back on the string," Bennie explained.

"Okay, I ready my mace then," said Tamara. "And raise my shield."

"I'll cast—" said Theo.

"No, you don't have to fight," interrupted Kim. "The troll is under the command of a magic user. It picks up the massive bar from near the gate and lifts it into place."

"Where's the magic user?" asked Theo.

"She's high up on the wall above the gate, looking down. Altmoor, you can feel a kind of magic thread between her and the troll. But it is a magic well beyond you. For now. She's an elf, wearing silver robes and a broad-brimmed hat, and she has an oak staff with a giant ruby on the end."

"Okay," said Theo. "I'm going to call up to her. 'Excuse me, Lady Mage, can you direct us to the Town Wizard?'"

"You need to roll for the mage's reaction," said Kim. "Because you interrupted her it's minus one, but you were polite so plus one."

"And my charisma is fifteen," said Theo. He rolled the twenty-sided die. For a moment it teetered on becoming a one, and there was a microsecond of tension before it settled on eighteen.

"She likes you," said Kim.

"Phew," said Theo.

Kim cleared his throat, making his voice go high and what he hoped sounded elegant and powerful, acting out the role of the wizard. He heard Madir giggle behind him, but the players were not distracted.

"I am the Town Wizard, travelers," said Kim. "My name is Lelanthe. What do you want with me?"

Theo answered. Soon, Kim was totally engrossed, as the players delivered the scroll to Lelanthe and it turned out to be a curse, which she deflected. The players were arrested and there was a trial, and they were set a task to prove their innocence by capturing the old dwarf who'd given them the scroll in the inn back in Yender, and Kim managed to lose himself in the game, almost forgetting his troubles with Aster and Eila.

Almost, but not quite.

CHAPTER EIGHT

Four hours later, the session finished with the players delivering the old dwarf (who turned out to be a priest of an anti-elf god called Tickrock) in chains to Lelanthe. They'd earned enough experience to level up, from two to three, and sorting all that out took another hour, with pencils hard at work on character sheets, and lots of erasing and rewriting.

Normally Bennie would have made tea and sandwiches for everyone halfway through the game, but she had said it wasn't okay to go into the house until her parents woke up. When Kim suggested they send Madir in to get snacks, Bennie frowned and said that wouldn't be a good idea. So everyone was starving when they finished, though they at least had glasses of water.

"I have to go home and eat something," said Kim.

"Yeah, me too," said Theo. "See you. Thanks for the game."

He left, with Tamara following. They usually hung out together. In the last year, people had started making jokes about them being boyfriend and girlfriend. A few brave people had said that about Bennie and Kim too, but not when Bennie could hear, in case she didn't like it and took her usual direct action. Kim wasn't sure how he felt about this. He'd been friends with Bennie forever, and the idea of them being something different was troubling, even as he felt that things were changing. He tried not to think about it.

"You want to come to our place?" Kim asked Bennie. "Dad made bread this morning, and there's cheese. And Vegemite."

"Nah," said Bennie. Darwin's wholemeal bread might be very healthy, but it was heavy and took ages to chew. "Mad and I might go down to the shops. I've got money."

"I'm going out with Eila soon," said Madir.

"Oh yeah?" asked Kim. "Where?"

"Secret," said Madir, with a shrug.

"Okay, see if I care." Kim was slightly worried about what they might be getting up to, but also pleased. If Eila went out with Madir in the daytime, then he could search her room and find the globe. "Oh, yeah, Bennie, can I borrow your big net? The prawning one you use down the coast?"

"What for?" asked Bennie.

"I'll tell you later," said Kim, with a sideways glance at Madir.

"See if I care," parroted Bennie's sister.

"If you're responsible, you can borrow it," said Bennie. "Granddad gave it to me, and I'll get in big trouble if you break it, or tear the net or anything. I'll need it for the summer holidays."

The prawning net was a proper bit of gear, an aluminium pole with a heavy-duty nylon mesh net that was big enough to fit the globe. Bennie's grandparents lived down on the South Coast, and Bennie and Madir usually spent all the long summer holidays with them, and nighttime prawning in the nearby lagoon was a regular activity. But their parents didn't go with them—they were always too busy with their work.

Madir left as Bennie rummaged around the back of the garage, eventually returning with the net.

"So what do you want this for?"

"To pick up the globe," said Kim. "So I don't have to touch it and risk it getting at my mind. I'm going to chuck it back in the lake."

"Why?" asked Bennie.

"*Why?* You felt it trying to get into your head, didn't you? You couldn't even let go until I dragged you away."

"I was about to let go," said Bennie, though not with much conviction. "But it doesn't seem to have done Eila any harm."

"She's sneaking out at night and the globe killed a ton of ants. She calls it Aster, by the way. Says that's the closest to its name we can say."

"It killed a ton of ants?"

Kim explained what he'd seen, and also the weirdness of Eila being so interested in the injured kangaroo.

"That doesn't mean anything," said Bennie. "We killed a lot of ants last year, freezing them."

"About twenty," Kim protested. "And some of them survived. The globe thing must have killed a couple thousand. And the other ants wouldn't touch the bodies."

He and Bennie had tried putting ants in suspended animation, freezing them and then giving them shocks from a nine-volt battery. Sometimes the ants revived, sometimes they didn't. Eila had said it was an unscientific experiment, as they weren't keeping proper records, and they had lost interest soon after that.

"I think there's still some ants in the freezer here, come to think of it," said Bennie. "Look, there's billions of ants around. There's probably a million in that ant nest. A few thousand is no big deal."

"I don't like it," said Kim stubbornly. "And there's this weird cloud overhead. I bet Aster's got something to do with that as well."

"What weird cloud?" asked Bennie.

They had to go outside for Bennie to look up. Kim thought the circular cloud had spread a little farther since that morning, but it was hard to tell. It had thickened up, he was sure about that, and it was the only cloud up there, covering the city with the sky beyond completely blue and clear.

"Looks like any other cloud to me," said Bennie. "Except for the weird shape."

"Mrs. Benison said it wasn't normal," replied Kim. "I think Aster's got something to do with it."

But Bennie wasn't listening to him. She had turned her head toward her house. Two people were shouting inside. Bennie's parents. As far as Kim could hear, they were arguing about whose job was more important and blaming each other for being away.

"I'll come with you," said Bennie. "Give you a hand."

Kim started to say something about the shouting, but didn't. Everyone knew Bennie's parents not only spent very little time at home, but didn't get along with each other when they were there. But Bennie and Madir never wanted to talk about it.

Bennie went back for her bike, got on, and took off straightaway, riding fast uphill, her head down. He raced over to get on his own bike, holding the prawning net over his shoulder, steering with one hand, which was always tempting fate with the old bicycle.

They went in through the front gate of the farm, since Kim knew his parents probably wouldn't give him a job to do if Bennie was with him. They liked Bennie and thought she was a good influence. But he needn't have worried, since neither his father nor mother were at the house. He could hear hammering in the distance and remembered they were both going to be working on fixing up a trellis in greenhouse five, the second farthest from the house. Well out of the way.

"So we just get that globe thing and take it straight down to the lake and chuck it in?" asked Bennie. After dropping their bikes in the shed, they'd gone to Kim's room first, to drop off his Dungeons & Dragons stuff disguised among the school books.

"I guess so," replied Kim. Now that it came to it, his fear of what Aster might be able to do had returned in force. Perhaps those icy tendrils could reach into his brain even without him touching the globe?

"Well, if that's what you want to do, let's do it," said Bennie with a shrug. Kim knew she was afraid too, but she would never admit to fear. Her way of dealing with fear was to tackle whatever caused it straight on. Except her parents, he suddenly thought. Bennie avoided even talking about what was going on with them.

"Yeah, let's go," he said, brandishing the prawning net. He held it up in front of him as they approached Eila's room. Bennie opened the door and stood to one side, taking cover like in a cop show. Kim jumped in and looked around, ready to sweep the globe up into the net.

But he couldn't see it. The room was dark, the curtain drawn tight across the window. Kim turned on the light and looked around.

Eila's room was as tidy as ever. Her desk held three piles of books, each no more than four volumes high. There was one book by itself in the middle of the desk. Kim looked closer and saw it was from the public library and was for adults, not children. It was called *An Introduction to Weather Systems*. There was an open notebook next to it, with some sketches involving arrows and clouds. Kim looked at it for a few seconds, thinking.

Several of the other books were also about the weather, and the rest were medical textbooks. University-level texts, for scientists and doctors. This wasn't unusual for Eila; she always read many years in advance of her actual age. But she hadn't been interested in weather before. Or medicine and biology.

Eila's bed was properly made up, much more carefully than Kim's. He checked her wardrobe, sliding the doors open to show neatly arranged clothes hanging inside. The globe was not tucked away beneath them.

"It's not here," Kim proclaimed with a sigh.

"Under the bed?" suggested Bennie. She stepped into the room warily and looked around.

Kim got down on his stomach to look. He saw the basketball immediately, right up the end. A faint spark appeared on its surface, slowly growing brighter until it was a brilliant red circle, the size of a thumbnail. It was as if Aster had opened an eye and was watching him. Then the light slowly faded, and it was just an old basketball again.

"Yeah, it's here," he said. "I'm going to use the net to roll it out."

There wasn't enough room under the bed to get the actual net over the globe, so Kim reversed it and poked the globe with the staff, planning to push it out. But it wasn't like trying to lever out a normal basketball. The globe hardly moved, like it was made of something really heavy, solid metal or stone. Far too heavy for Eila to have carried it home from the lake.

"It's made itself heavy somehow," said Kim with a grunt.

He exerted more force, using both hands on the staff. Slowly the ball began to roll out from under the bed. *Very* slowly, with Kim needing to use all his strength to keep it going. It didn't roll easily at all, not like it should.

"Here it comes—"

A blinding, crackling bolt of electricity leaped from the globe, along the aluminium shaft of the net and straight into Kim. He was thrown backward, crashing into the wall.

Shocked, pale, and gasping for breath, he could only watch as the globe rolled itself back under the bed.

CHAPTER NINE

"Are you sure you're okay?" asked Bennie.

"Yes," coughed Kim. "I just couldn't breathe for a few seconds."

They were back in Kim's room, at least temporarily defeated. Bennie had dragged Kim out and helped him up, but he was able to walk on his own after a few seconds.

"Have to get it out with wooden sticks," mused Bennie. "Or maybe a hose looped over or something like that. Whatever won't conduct electricity."

"A hockey stick," contributed Kim.

"You got one?"

"No," said Kim. He thought for a few seconds. "The big outside broom! That's all wood. I'll get it."

"No, you rest for a minute, I'll get it. Where is it?"

"Should be inside the big shed," replied Kim. "To the right as you go in the front, near the bikes."

"Got it," Bennie said and ran out.

Kim sat on his bed and thought about the sudden weight of the globe. Even if they rolled it out from under the bed, how would they get it down to the lake?

And what else could it do if they touched it, besides the electric shocks and the mind control?

Bennie was back far too quickly for Kim's liking. She had the big outdoor broom, which was taller than she was, and the brush end with its thick bristles was as long as Kim's arm.

"Let me get it out this time," said Bennie when Kim reached for the broom.

"It might be able to do something else," Kim warned quietly. "More than electric shocks, I mean."

"We'll find out," said Bennie, undeterred. "Come on."

They went back into Eila's room. Bennie crouched down and looked under the bed.

"Oh man! It's got a creepy kind of red eye . . . No, it just went out. Or closed."

She slid the broom under the bed and positioned the brush behind the globe. When she hauled back on it, the globe once again hardly moved. Kim knelt to help her, and with both of them pulling hard they managed to slide it out from under the bed.

"Okay," Kim said with relief. "We've got it!"

As if in response, the globe suddenly rolled toward them, wreathed in electric sparks. Bennie jumped back, cannoning into Kim, who caught her, and then somehow they managed to use the broom to push the globe back against the wall and hold it there, though it took all their strength. The sparking lines of electrical fire around it ebbed away, but the globe kept pushing against the broom.

"What do we do now?" panted Bennie. "How does it move on its own?"

"It has a mind," said Kim. "That's how."

"Very scientific," snapped Bennie. "Hold it! Hold it!"

They both leaned in, pushing hard.

The broomstick snapped in half, and the globe rolled demonically toward them, tumbling over the broken piece. Crackling sparks spat out again, looking for connection.

Bennie got through the door a second after Kim, who pulled it shut behind them. The door boomed like thunder as the globe rammed it, but held firm. The crackle of electricity stopped, followed by an ominous silence.

They held the door closed, their hands overlapping on the handle, gripping it tight.

"What if it gets out the window?" asked Bennie urgently. "Is it going to hunt us down?"

"I don't know," said Kim. "We need—"

"What are you doing?" asked Eila. She stood at the other end of the hall, holding a cardboard shoebox with air holes punched in it. Madir was behind her, holding an identical box.

"Saving ourselves from *your* demon globe thing," snapped Bennie. "Can it get out the window?"

"Did you open the window? Or the curtain?" asked Eila urgently.

"No!" said Kim. "Can it get out on its own?"

"Don't be silly," said Eila. She seemed relieved, though no one but Kim would have noticed the slight change in her expression.

"Silly! That globe monster electrocuted Kim and it rolls around of its own accord," yelled Bennie.

"She won't do anything if you leave her alone," Eila replied calmly.

"Are you sure?" asked Kim.

"Yes. Without my instructions, Aster can only act in self-defense."

"Your instructions? So you *could* tell it to hunt us down and electrocute us?" asked Bennie.

Eila hesitated, then nodded slowly.

"I suppose I could," she said. "But I wouldn't. If you leave Aster alone, she'll leave you alone. *We'll* leave you alone."

Bennie looked at Kim. Kim looked at Bennie. They saw deep uneasiness in each other's eyes.

"Eila, it's too dangerous. We have to tell Mum and Dad," said Kim. "We need to—"

"Tell us what?" asked Darwin, who had just come in. He was barefoot, having taken off his gum boots outside, and was holding his very dirty hands up so he remembered to not touch anything before he washed them. He looked like he was surrendering to someone, except he was advancing like someone who was about to take a surrender, not give one.

Kim whirled around, letting go of the door handle. So did Bennie. Eila handed the box she was holding to Madir in a superswift move.

Kim knew he had a difficult choice to make. In matters where it was his word against Eila's, his parents almost always took Eila's side. But the danger—and the proof—was hiding right in Eila's room. He had to say something.

"Dad, Eila found a—"

"Basketball in the lake," Eila interrupted, opening the door to her bedroom. Sure enough, there was the old basketball.

"Who broke the broom?" asked Darwin crossly. "That's farm property."

"Kim and Bennie did," said Eila. "Playing some sort of game with the ball that I found, when I said they couldn't have it."

"That's not what happened!" protested Kim. Bennie was silent next to him, her head down.

"Did you break the broom?" asked Darwin, looking hard at his son.

"Uh, I guess we did," said Kim. "But, Dad, that ball isn't just a basketball—"

"You do know that every time anything that belongs to the farm is broken I have to fill out three forms to get a replacement? Three forms! And I *hate* forms!"

"I'll help you, Dad," Eila volunteered. "I like forms."

Kim wasn't sure which was worse—the way Eila was going to get away with this or actual electric shocks.

"No, that's okay—I have to do it," said Darwin with a sigh. "Kim, be more careful, please. And don't play with Eila's things if she doesn't give you permission. Understood?"

Kim wanted to protest, but he knew it was useless. The globe would stay a basketball, and he couldn't prove it was anything else.

He nodded slowly.

"Yes," he said.

"And what do you say to your sister?"

You're nothing but trouble, Kim thought. But instead he said, "Sorry, Eila."

"Right," said Darwin. "I've got to get cleaned up. Take

those pieces back to the shed, Kim. Maybe I can make a new broomstick so I don't have to bother with any forms. Nice to see you, Bennie. Madir."

"You too, Mr. Basalt," the two of them chorused.

"Call me Darwin!" said Kim's father as he walked away. He always said that, but Bennie and Madir never called him anything but "Mr. Basalt." They called their own father "Sir."

"What have you got there?" asked Bennie, gesturing to the boxes in Madir's hands.

"Guinea pigs," said Madir, holding them up. "Mine's called Lisa, and Eila's hasn't got a name. Kelly Phipson is giving them away. She bought two at a church fete last month, and now she's got heaps."

"They were both meant to be male," said Eila. "But obviously not."

"Mum and Dad won't let you keep a guinea pig," said Bennie.

"I'll hide her in the garage," said Madir. "They won't know."

"I don't think our parents will let you keep one either," said Kim to Eila. Although at this point he wondered: If Eila brought an elephant to stay with them, would their parents be okay with it, because they were okay with anything she did?

"It won't be a problem," said Eila.

Easy for you to say, Kim thought.

"Enough about guinea pigs!" he told his sister. "That globe—Aster or whatever you want to call it—did try to electrocute me. It could have killed me! I don't trust it. Eila, you have to—"

Eila cut him off coldly. "I don't have to do anything. I told you, Aster will leave you alone if you leave her alone. That's it. Come on, Madir."

Madir gave Kim and Bennie a disdainful look and went into the bedroom. Eila followed, and shut the door behind her. A few seconds later, she opened it again, handed Kim the two pieces of the broom, and Bennie the prawning net, and shut it firmly again.

"Well, we tried," said Bennie.

She shrugged, as if shaking off the whole thing.

Kim did not shrug. He felt deep in his heart that something *had* to be done about Aster.

But what?

CHAPTER TEN

Monday morning was gloomy, and it wasn't because Kim had to go to school. The cloud overhead had spread farther and gotten thicker, so there was no direct sunshine.

His parents remarked on it at breakfast while Kim and Eila were still eating their homemade granola. It usually took quite a while to get it down, as every component was so chewy.

"Very unusual cloud formation overhead," said Darwin. "Some sort of inversion effect, I would say."

"It'll disperse later," said Marie confidently, lowering the newspaper she was reading. She read the daily paper all the way through every morning, occasionally passing it over to Darwin for him to read a particular article. Kim peeked at the headlines, wondering if there was any mention of strange things happening in town, but it was just all the usual boring local news.

Eila didn't glance at the paper once. It was almost like she already knew all the news.

"They can hang on for days," said Darwin. "Though admittedly not usually so far from the sea. I don't think the lake is big enough to have the same sort of effect, though I suppose it is a new factor in the microclimate."

The lake had been created by damming a river, and had only filled up about ten years before. There was a photograph of Marie and baby Kim looking out over the rabbit-infested fields that became the lake later that year, with the three small hills that became islands in front of them.

"What if it's not natural?" asked Kim. Eila turned to him and scowled fleetingly, an expression so swift their parents missed it.

"What do you mean?" asked Darwin. "An inversion layer is a known meteorological phenomenon. It certainly isn't bushfire smoke or some other kind of human pollution."

"Unusual, but not unprecedented," confirmed Marie. "Finish up, you two—you have to leave in five minutes."

"I'll need your help for an hour after school, Kim," Darwin added. "The watering system in greenhouse four has got a leak somewhere; it needs to be tracked down."

Kim groaned. That meant crawling along in the narrow space between two lines of raised garden beds and following the hoses until he found a patch of mud or some obvious leak. His father was too big to fit between the beds, so Kim had to do it.

"Or there's a hundred bags of horse manure being delivered today that'll need stacking," continued Darwin. "Would you prefer to help me with that?"

"No, no," said Kim hastily. "I'll find the leak."

He finished his granola and hurried away, sneaking a look at Eila as he went past. He'd heard her go out again in the night but hadn't followed. He told himself it was because he'd been too tired, but he knew it was because he was afraid. Everything was more frightening at night, in the dark. He could too easily remember the feeling of that electric shock, of being thrown back and made breathless and weak.

He didn't want to imagine that happening somewhere out in the darkness, without Bennie to drag him away.

As always, Kim rode his bike to school, stopping briefly at Bennie's house. She was ready, and they went on together. Also as per usual, Eila rode behind Kim, but she had to wait longer for Madir, so the younger pair were almost out of sight when Kim and Bennie arrived at the school and parked their bikes in the racks. Bennie locked hers up, but Kim didn't bother. No one had ever tried to steal his bike.

"The cloud is thicker," said Kim gloomily as they walked inside. "I'm sure Aster's doing it."

"Forget about the globe," said Bennie. "Eila's right. We should have left it alone."

"It's evil," said Kim.

"You don't know that. Life isn't D and D. You can't cast a Detect Evil spell. And Eila said Aster won't do anything bad."

"Not exactly," said Kim quietly. They had joined the line outside the classroom and other people could hear. "Eila told us the globe will do what she tells it to do."

"So?" asked Bennie. "That's okay, isn't it?"

"Maybe," said Kim doubtfully. "Eila's always so certain she knows what's right, but . . ."

"She is super smart," said Bennie.

"Yeah," replied Kim. "But she's still ten."

"You want to go up the Dipper after school?" asked Bennie, clearly tired of the subject of Eila and the globe.

"Won't have time," said Kim despondently. "I have to crawl around in between the garden beds in greenhouse four looking for leaks."

"I'll help!" said Bennie. "We can be explorers. It is kind of a maze. There might be giant rats and snakes."

"There might actually be snakes." Kim was much less excited about this than his friend was.

There *were* sometimes snakes in the greenhouses,

usually because a scientist had forgotten to close the doors, which the family never did. It was a very serious offense in the Basalt family to leave a greenhouse door open; Kim hadn't done it since he was six or seven. The snakes liked the warmth, so they were always keen to get in, except at the height of summer, when it was too hot.

Darwin picked the snakes up if they were hanging around somewhere they'd cause trouble. He had a special snake-handling gripper, a kind of rope-operated claw on the end of a long pole. He'd grip them near the head and drop them in a sack, then take them over to the government research center. Most were small black snakes, highly venomous but not usually aggressive. They had to be taken seriously, and Kim knew to avoid them.

"We'll need knives," said Bennie. "To fight the snakes."

"What?" asked Kim. Bennie, like everyone else who ever went up the mountain or into the bush, was well aware if you left the snakes alone they'd leave you alone. The only danger was if you accidentally trod on one. Or were stupid enough to try and attack one with a knife.

"Imaginary knives," said Bennie, doing some fancy air knife moves that culminated in her plunging a blade into Kim's chest, her closed fist just touching his breastbone. "For fighting imaginary snakes. Not the real ones."

"Oh, right. Okay, then," said Kim. He started to mime dying, his knees buckling and a gargling sound rising in his throat. He only stopped when Mrs. Thompson popped out of the classroom and ordered everyone in.

The rest of the school day was uneventful. Kim even managed to forget about the problem of Aster for a while, except at recess and lunch, when he went outside and saw the cloud overhead. It was definitely thicker and more widespread.

There was the usual rush to get out when the bell rang at 3:25. Being lordly sixth graders, Kim and Bennie let everyone rush past to the bike racks before claiming their own and slowly riding out after the majority of the horde had departed. Almost every kid at school rode a bike or walked; very few got picked up by their parents.

Kim had hoped his dad might have gotten distracted by the horse manure and forgotten about the leaking watering system. But he hadn't. He was waiting for Kim, and welcomed Bennie's offer of additional help.

Within a few minutes they were all in greenhouse four, which, like the others, was basically a really long steel-framed shed with walls and a roof made entirely of glass. It was heated in winter, but even without the heating on now, it was hot, the sun beating down through the glass.

There was a concrete floor in the space between the raised garden beds, but it was always covered with spilled earth and potting mixture, so it was very dirty work. Eventually Kim did find a big patch of mud caused by a leak, and he got even dirtier and muddier having to cut out the bad section of hose and replace it, involving considerable use of a very bad-smelling glue under his father's direction.

Bennie had helped search for the leak properly for a while, but soon started crawling around just for the fun of it, practicing fighting nonexistent snakes with imaginary swords and knives at first, then escalating to larger weapons with their own sound effects: machine guns, bombs, and, one of her favorites, a hissing that indicated a death ray.

"Right, that's done," said Darwin at last. He turned down the pocket radio he usually put on when he was working, though he only ever listened to informative shows, never music. The tinny voice that had been going on about molluscs faded away. "Now, let's see, there are a few other small jobs—"

"Uh, Dad, Bennie's here. Can't I do them tomorrow?"

Darwin hesitated, and looked over at Bennie.

"The work's got to be done, Kim," he said. "But I suppose

there's nothing urgent. You up to date on your homework?"

"Yes," said Kim. This was even true, though he would have said yes if it wasn't, trusting that he could catch up later. As long as his teachers didn't complain or give him less than a B on any subject, his parents wouldn't look too closely into when he was doing his homework, or how. Which was just as well, as he usually did Bennie's English homework and she did his math.

"What are you up to, then?" asked Darwin. But Kim knew it wasn't a real question. His father was already thinking about his own next job, looking at the blue notebook where he wrote down all the tasks for the day, the week, the month, and the year.

"Going up the mountain on our bikes," replied Kim. "Bennie! We can go!"

Bennie popped up from behind a garden bed right in front of Kim, making him jump.

"I was sneaking up on you," she said, miming a sword thrust. "You didn't notice me, right?"

"No," said Kim. "Come on. Let's go up the Dipper."

CHAPTER ELEVEN

They only made it to the lower embankment of the storm-water drain. There was a weird, off-putting gray furry lump there, like a discarded rug piled up on one spot. It stank, and there were ants all over it, a thick, moving carpet of ants. Kim dropped his bike and walked closer, but not too close. Bennie followed. Both of them knew there was something very wrong.

"What is it?" asked Bennie.

"A kangaroo, I think," said Kim slowly. "With all its bones removed."

"What?! How?"

Kim tilted his head, trying to make sense of what he was seeing. It was a lump of kangaroo fur with flesh inside, but there was no shape to it. There was no blood either. But the red ants were carrying away tiny pieces of meat. Thousands and thousands, tens of thousands of ants, far more than would normally swarm over a dead animal.

"I think it's the kangaroo Eila was looking at yesterday," he said. "The injured one."

"But how can it have no bones?"

"I don't know," said Kim. "But I bet Aster did it." He paused, swallowed, and then added, "I mean Aster and Eila."

"It was going to die, anyway," said Bennie. "I mean, maybe it was already dead when they did whatever they did to it."

Kim stepped back. Bennie quickly followed him. They retreated to their bikes, away from the smell.

"We have to get rid of the globe," Kim said.

"How?" asked Bennie. "It can make itself heavy, it's got that electric shock power, and it can move by itself."

"Yeah, it won't be easy," Kim conceded.

"Besides, if we chuck it in the lake it will just roll itself back out."

Kim hadn't thought of that.

"Or it will tell Eila to come get it," Bennie continued. "In her head."

"Telepathy," Kim groaned. "We'll have to destroy it somehow. Like Frodo and the ring."

"We haven't got a handy volcano," said Bennie. She'd only read *The Lord of the Rings* once, a few months back, at Kim's urging, but was just as much a fan.

"Maybe we could break it with a sledgehammer," said Kim.

"I doubt it. If it can make itself heavy or light, it would easily be able to change to resist anything physical. Probably even a bullet."

"Makes sense," said Kim despondently. "But it must have a weakness. Everything has a weakness."

"In stories," said Bennie.

"In life too," Kim swore.

They stood in silence for a while, both thinking. Finally, Bennie spoke.

"Those ants are really going for it. There's like a river of them going up and down."

Kim looked where Bennie pointed. There was a flowing river of ants, a thick red thread leading from the kangaroo lump downhill. To the farm. All carrying away lumps of flesh and fur, new ants coming up to strip away more.

"Oh," said Kim, realization hitting him. "The globe must have worked out how to control the ants. They're removing the evidence. Eila told me some of them dying was just part of Aster learning about them. I didn't understand she meant the globe was learning how to *control* them. I guess that's what happened to the kangaroo as well. And something went wrong."

"Why would the globe want to control kangaroos? That's not a big deal. They're not, like, lions or anything—"

"Don't you get it? Aster's working her way up. We'll be next."

"You and me?"

"Humans," said Kim.

"You're just guessing," said Bennie weakly.

"Yeah. But I bet I'm right."

"Eila said if we leave it . . . Aster . . . alone, she'll leave us alone."

Kim didn't think leaving it alone was an option. "We have to work out how to get rid of the globe," he insisted.

"Look, maybe Eila's right about it being basically harmless," said Bennie. "I mean, so there's some dead ants and a boneless kangaroo, and it's cloudy when maybe it shouldn't be . . . That's not the end of the world. We should leave it alone."

Kim shook his head.

"Kim! We can't do anything. Forget about the globe. All right?"

Kim didn't answer. Bennie would never admit to being afraid of anything. But now the fear was coming through. Kim knew there was no point in forcing the issue. He understood why Bennie was afraid—but he also felt disappointed that Bennie wasn't going to help him.

"No point hanging around here," Bennie went on, probably sensing Kim's disappointment but not wanting to look at it head-on. "Let's ride along the drain. Go over to Death Alley."

Death Alley was a steep concrete footpath that ran through a park on one of the foothills on the eastern side of the mountain, about a mile away. It had a sharp turn at the bottom, so riding down at full speed, it was easy to lose control and slide out. Since you slid on the grass, it wasn't *too* dangerous.

"No, thanks," Kim answered stiffly. "I already grazed my knees the other day. I have to work out what to do."

"Okay." Bennie hesitated, then said gruffly, "I guess I should just go home."

They rode down in silence and were almost back at the farm when they saw Eila and Madir at the corner of the perimeter fence, by the big tree and the ant nest. Madir was hunched over and sobbing.

Bennie swerved off the track and accelerated, zooming over to the tree, coming to a stop in a side-on skid. She dropped the bike and rushed to the fence, peering through it at Madir.

"Mad! What's wrong?"

"Lisa died," said Madir. Seeing the incomprehension on Bennie's face, she showed her the empty shoebox she held. "My guinea pig. And Eila's died too."

"Did it?" said Kim sarcastically, as he rode up. He glared through the mesh fencing at Eila, who did not look his way. "Just like that?"

"We're giving the guinea pigs to the ants," said Madir. "Like a funeral. For heroes, because they died for science."

"Did Aster kill them, Eila?" asked Kim fiercely. "And the kangaroo. What did she do to it?"

Eila took a deep breath and turned to her brother.

"Aster's still learning," she said. "I wanted her to heal the kangaroo. I thought she knew enough from the guinea pigs, but it went wrong."

"So she *did* kill the guinea pigs as well?"

"Aster didn't kill them *on purpose*," said Eila. "It was my idea to see if we could heal the kangaroo. Anyway, guinea pigs are often used in scientific experiments. You know, that's where the expression 'being a guinea pig' comes from. All the rest of Kelly's guinea pigs have gone to the government lab. What I tried is no different."

"But Madir's was a pet!" exclaimed Bennie. "She gave it a name!"

"Lisa," said Madir. She rubbed her eyes. "Eila told me Lisa might not make it. I knew. Aster needs to know how animals work inside."

"Why?" asked Kim.

"She wants to learn," said Eila. "And I know she can help us. I told you before."

"Help us how?"

"Different ways. Depending on the problem. Look, you don't need to worry. Leave Aster alone. Leave me alone."

"Yeah," added Madir.

"Sounds sensible to me," said Bennie. She didn't look at Kim.

"There's nothing I can do, anyway," Kim pointed out bitterly. He wheeled his bike back away from the fence.

"See you at school," Bennie called out.

But Kim didn't answer, or look back.

CHAPTER TWELVE

The rest of the week passed in a blur for Kim. He hardly spoke to Bennie, something that had never happened before. He did his schoolwork, did his chores at home, did all his homework himself. He didn't sleep well, and several times woke up to hear Eila going out in the middle of the night. But he didn't follow her.

All the adults talked about the cloud more and more. His parents, the teachers, the scientists who came to the farm, everyone. But they all still accepted it as a bizarre natural phenomenon and expected it to eventually dissipate or blow away.

Kim expected it to get thicker and more widespread. So he was astonished when he went out on Friday morning to go to school and saw the sun shining in an almost entirely blue sky. There was only a small remnant of the cloud, lurking directly above the mountain. It was about one-tenth the size it had been the night before, and it was coming apart, wisps trailing off and blowing away.

Eila was already outside, with her bike. She was looking up at the sky.

"Something go wrong?" asked Kim.

Eila turned her head to look at him.

"With the cloud," Kim continued. "Aster was doing that, wasn't she?"

Eila nodded slowly. "An experiment I wanted her to try. But it was getting too much attention. And we learned what we need to know. Nothing for you to worry about, Kim."

Kim felt cursed to have a younger sister who treated him like he was five years old. It was infuriating.

"I *am* worried!" he shouted. "Why does Aster need it to be cloudy? Why can't she come out in the sun? She's like a vampire or something."

"Aster is nothing like a vampire," said Eila, her voice running as cold as Kim's ran hot. "There are no such things as vampires."

"So what's her problem with sunshine?"

Eila looked back up at the sky. "Aster has no problem with sunshine."

"Why don't you go get her, then?" asked Kim. "Bring her out. I've never seen her in the sun. You two always sneak around at night."

Eila sighed and returned her gaze to her brother. He didn't find it comfortable. Eila looked at him the same way she looked at the weeds she had to pull out of the carrot beds. "We have to go to school. Forget about Aster. You really don't have to worry about her, Kim."

"I wish I could forget her," grumbled Kim. "Can't you please, please, get rid of her?"

"She's my friend," said Eila. "I'm helping her learn. When she's learned enough, I'm going to get her to help us."

"Eila! Why not just check with some grown-ups about what you want to do? Talk to the scientists, tell them about Aster. How about Professor Lowton? You like her—"

"No," said Eila. "Aster doesn't want anyone to know about her, particularly adults. You really need to stop worrying, Kim. Aster is studying our world, that's all. We've learned all we need to know about the weather. The cloud won't come back."

"And the ants, and the kangaroo, and the guinea pigs—"

"We'll be late. You need to get going."

"I'll go after you. I don't care if I'm late."

"Don't try and do anything to Aster," warned Eila. "She is perfectly harmless, unless you do something that makes her defend herself."

"I'm not going to try anything. I really am going to school!" protested Kim. "I'm just letting you leave first."

Kim always left first. Eila followed a bit later. That's how it had always been.

"Bennie will be waiting for you," Eila pointed out.

"She can wait," Kim replied bitterly. "Go!"

Eila shrugged, got on her bike, and rode away.

Kim stood by his own bike, just holding the handlebars, looking up at the sky again. Maybe the fact that it had cleared was a good sign. He wished there was something he could do. He wished that Bennie would help him, or that he could make things be normal again.

His father came into the shed from the other side, carrying a tray of seedlings that would be picked up and taken by car to the university or the government laboratories.

"Kim! Why are you still here? You'll be late!"

"I know! I know!" Kim didn't know why he felt so angry. Angry and helpless. He got on his bike and rode off, with Darwin Basalt staring after him.

Bennie was still waiting for him, outside her house. Eila and Madir were already almost out of sight.

"Hey! You're late," said Bennie. "We'll have to race."

Kim grunted but did not speed up. Bennie rode around him in a circle.

"Come on!" she said. "It's assembly morning. You know you'll have to see the Skull if we get there after nine."

The Skull was their name for the deputy principal, who

had a very thin face and never smiled. All the kids were frightened of him, entirely based on how he looked. As far as Kim knew, he never actually did anything except loom up unexpectedly.

"You go," he said miserably. "I don't care if I have to see the Skull."

"Come on, Kim. Look up! The sky's blue, it's a beautiful day. Also I've got a surprise for you. A present."

Interest flickered through Kim's gloom.

"A present? It isn't my birthday."

"Yeah, well, it's kind of a present for me too." Bennie circled again and matched speed with Kim, but immediately started to speed up again. Instinctively, he did too. "And for Theo and Tamara."

"The D and D group?" asked Kim, now really interested. "What is it?"

"You'll see," said Bennie, speeding up again. "Lunchtime."

"Wait! What is it?" yelled Kim, standing up to pedal harder. It was always difficult for him to keep up on his heavy old bike when Bennie really went for it on her ten-speed.

They got to school at two minutes before nine, rushing in just in time for morning assembly, under the watchful gaze of the Skull.

All through the morning, Bennie refused to talk about whatever it was she'd got for Kim. Kim kept asking her about it, and before long they were talking together just like they always did, even getting into trouble from Mrs. Thompson, who made them move seats. Even at recess, Bennie wouldn't reveal what was coming, laughing at Kim's guesses of new dice, a practice sword, a wizard's hat, or the metal figurines they knew existed but had never seen.

Finally, at lunchtime, Bennie gathered Theo and Tamara, who from their smiles already knew what was coming. The four of them clustered under one of the big oak trees at the far end of the oval, where only the sixth graders were allowed to go.

Bennie produced a big manilla envelope and handed it to Kim.

"This is for all of us," she said. "But you'll look after it, Kim."

Kim knew instantly that it was D&D related. He could feel the shape of a book inside, the same size as the original rule books. But it was thicker. The flap of the envelope wasn't stuck down, so he flicked it back, reached in, and pulled out the most beautiful thing he had ever seen.

Greyhawk. A supplement to Dungeons & Dragons!

"I got it yesterday afternoon," said Bennie. "I went to the games shop after my dentist appointment and it was just there."

Kim flicked through the pages.

"There's a new kind of fighter called a paladin," he said, marveling. "And a thief class!"

"I read through it last night," said Bennie. "There are a ton of new monsters. And magic items. And spells."

"What's this thing on the cover?" asked Kim. "The floating globe with the tentacles?"

"They're not tentacles," Bennie explained. "They're eyes on stalks. Each eye can cast a different spell. It's called a Beholder."

Kim flicked through the book to find the entry.

"'Also called a Sphere of Many Eyes,'" he read. "'Or Eye Tyrant.' Like Aster, but with eyes . . ."

"Aster?" asked Theo.

"Oh, nothing," said Kim hurriedly, with a swift glance at Bennie. "Something in a story. This is amazing! Magic users have new spells, up to ninth level!"

"Let me see that!" exclaimed Theo, craning in closer.

"You don't get any ninth-level spells until you're level eighteen," cautioned Bennie.

"Wow, at the rate we've advanced so far, that's going to take, let's see . . ." Theo started to calculate but Tamara was quicker.

"Six years, playing forty out of fifty-two Sundays every year," she said. "We'll be in the last year of high school by then!"

"If we're still playing," said Kim. What he really meant was, *If Aster doesn't destroy us first.*

"Why wouldn't we be?" asked Bennie.

Kim was annoyed. Bennie was the only person there who should have known what he meant. But he wasn't going to get into it with Theo and Tamara listening. "Your characters would probably go up faster than they have been," he said. "I'm still working everything out, remember."

"So we're playing this Sunday?" asked Tamara.

Kim hesitated.

"We should," declared Bennie.

Kim tried to convince himself to be cheerful. The sky *had* cleared. The sunshine *was* warm. Maybe he didn't have to worry about Aster. He could stop fretting about his inability to do anything, and simply believe Eila when she said there was nothing to worry about. Even after only a few minutes rushing through *Greyhawk*, he had already seen monsters he wanted to use in the next adventure, and cool magic items, though he'd have to be careful not to overpower either the monsters or give too much to the players ...

"Yeah, yeah, I guess we should," he agreed. "Can we play at your place, Bennie?"

Bennie's cheerful face clouded for a moment.

"I guess," she said. "In the garage, anyway."

Before anyone could ask why, she added quickly, wanting to get it over, "My parents had a big fight about who had the more important work trip to go on, and they couldn't agree, so both have stayed home and they're both furious."

"Maybe they'll—" Theo started to say, but Bennie shook her head firmly even as he spoke, cutting off any further conversation on that topic.

Kim spent the rest of lunchtime reading *Greyhawk*, with the others reading along over his shoulder, clustered close. He was tempted to try to read it in class, but the fear it might be confiscated outweighed the temptation, so he kept it in his bag.

The sky was still clear after school—even the remnant cloud above the mountain had disappeared. Kim felt lighter, relieved. Maybe Bennie was right, Aster was basically harmless. He didn't need to try and do anything about her. He could rush through whatever jobs he was given and get back to reading *Greyhawk* and working out the adventure for Sunday.

Life could be good again.

CHAPTER THIRTEEN

Kim's detour into cheerfulness continued through the beginning of the weekend. The sky had remained clear, he and Bennie were talking again, his parents didn't give him any more jobs than usual, and, best of all, he had *Greyhawk* to pore through for the Sunday game.

He'd even been able to sleep through Eila's nighttime excursions, if she had any. He thought he'd heard her go out the night before, but he didn't really wake up properly, and in the morning he wasn't sure if he'd dreamed it. Perhaps, he told himself, nothing was going to happen with the globe. He'd leave Aster alone, and everything would be okay.

But then Sunday morning came along.

"There you are, Kim," said his mother, suddenly appearing in the doorway of his room while Kim was at his desk. Kim started, and resisted the urge to cover up the plan of the dungeon he was drawing on graph paper.

"What are you working on?" she asked.

"A plan of the great pyramid," replied Kim. This was true as far as it went; he *was* drawing a plan of *a* great pyramid . . . which just happened to be on top of a dungeon and didn't have anything to do with ancient Egypt.

"History can teach us some useful lessons," said Marie. "I don't want to interrupt your homework, but I need you to take some bread and soup up to Mrs. Benison. I've heard she isn't doing well."

"Bread and soup?" asked Kim. "How can I take soup up the mountain? Can't one of the scientists—"

"I've put the soup in a thermos. You can carry it and the bread in your school backpack."

"I'm meant to be at Bennie's by eleven," said Kim. "You said that was okay."

"And it is okay," replied Marie. "Luckily it's only half past nine now. You can get up the mountain and back if you don't waste time."

Kim opened his mouth to protest but shut it again without saying anything. He knew that expression on his mother's face. If he complained now, he would not be going to Bennie's. He'd be chipping mortar off old bricks all afternoon instead.

He also felt a bit ashamed by his first response. If Mrs. Benison wasn't well, then he should take her soup and bread and not complain. Only it would be so much easier if someone with a car did the delivering . . .

It was hotter than the last time he'd walked up the mountain. There was no cloud at all, and already the beginning of summer heat was starting to take effect. Kim had to rest twice on the way up.

When he finally got to Mrs. Benison's house, he saw the white government car parked outside. Mrs. Benison's granddaughter must be visiting. Kim sighed. It would have been so much easier if his mother had just called her to drop in and pick up the bread and soup on her way. But then they didn't have a telephone.

He crossed the veranda and used the old cast-iron knocker to rap three times. While he was waiting, he put his bag down by his feet, opened it, and got out the thermos and the loaf of bread, holding them ready to hand over. A quick transfer, and he'd be away down the mountain.

He heard footsteps, and the door opened. It wasn't Mrs. Benison. It was a tall, wiry woman older than Kim's parents. She was in full-dress police uniform, complete with medals, crowns on her epaulettes, blue trousers with a dark blue line down the outside, and very shiny black shoes.

"Um," said Kim, rather taken aback. She looked like she was about to lead a parade. He held up the thermos and the hefty loaf, and felt a strange urge to identify himself and give a reason for being there, because she was a police officer. "Um, I've brought some soup and bread for Mrs. Benison. I'm Kim Basalt."

"Right, you're from the family at the experimental farm," said the woman. "I'm Sheree Benison. But you can call me Chief Inspector. Or ma'am."

"Yes, ma'am," stammered Kim.

"I'm joking!" said the woman. "Call me Sheree. Grandma's told me about your family and your kind gifts. Come on in. She's in the library."

Kim's eyebrows went up. He didn't know Mrs. Benison had a library! He had only ever seen the front hall and the kitchen, and he'd once looked into the front living room through the windows on the veranda.

He followed Chief Inspector Benison along the hall to a door on the left, which he'd never seen open before.

"Grandma!" she called. "It's Kim Basalt, and he's brought you bread and soup!"

She turned to Kim, and took the bread and thermos, carefully holding both away from herself, wary of crumbs and spillage. "I'll take these into the kitchen. Go on in."

Kim obeyed, went through the door, and stopped, awestruck.

Mrs. Benison had a *real* library, the sort of place Kim had only read about in books. It was a large room, bigger than the kitchen, and every wall had floor-to-ceiling bookshelves, with a ladder to reach the higher titles. There were two high-backed leather armchairs near the single window in the rear, with a small table between them. The table had a teetering pile of six or seven books on top of it, and on top of the pile was Mrs. Benison's favorite tea mug.

Mrs. Benison was in the left-hand chair. She didn't look sick to Kim—she looked like she always did, bright-eyed and cheerful. She put the book she was reading down in her lap and waved to him.

"Hello, Kim! Come in. What's going on? You look like a spooked cat."

"I didn't know you had a library," explained Kim. He took a few steps in, looking all around him in awe. There were so many books!

"I didn't know you'd be interested," said Mrs. Benison. "Are you a reader?"

Kim nodded energetically.

"What kinds of books do you like to read?"

"Everything. Stories mostly, I guess." He hesitated, then added, "But my parents don't let . . . don't like me . . . to read fiction. But I do."

"Not read fiction!" exclaimed Mrs. Benison. "How awful

for you. And for them. Stories are how we experience other people's lives and loves, challenges, triumphs, and, I daresay, defeats and how to get past them. Take this book I'm reading now. Through it, I am experiencing what it would be like to live in the American South, and in it I have met a number of people who I love and admire, and can visit with every time I read the book. And it is a story of injustice, and of hatred, but also of love and redemption."

"What's it called?" asked Kim, walking closer.

"*To Kill a Mockingbird*," replied Mrs. Benison. "An American friend of my husband's gave it to us many years ago, but even then it was already a very famous book all around the world. There is an excellent film of it too, which I recommend."

"I've hardly seen any films," said Kim. "Only a few at school. My parents don't . . ."

"Ah yes," replied Mrs. Benison. "And no television at home. Eila told me that."

"Eila did?" asked Kim. As far as he knew, Eila had never even met Mrs. Benison. "When?"

"She came to see me last night," replied the old lady. "I was a little surprised to see a child up here so late, until she explained."

"Last night?" Kim couldn't believe what he was hearing. "How . . . what . . ."

"She quite cheered me up," continued Mrs. Benison. "In fact, I had been feeling rather ill, but her visit made me feel so much better."

"How did she explain being here so late?" asked Kim. He felt a sudden weight in his middle, a ball of apprehension and dread. What had Eila done?

"It was kind of her to leave the stargazing excursion to visit," replied Mrs. Benison. "Your family have been very kind to me, Kim. I appreciate your visits, and kind gifts."

"The stargazing excursion?"

"Yes, up to the summit. They won't be able to see the stars when the new tower's built—I expect it will have floodlights all over it. Eila sounds very keen on your school's astronomy club."

Kim was positive there was no astronomy club at school.

He began to tell Mrs. Benison this but was interrupted by her granddaughter, who strode into the room and thrust the now-empty thermos into his hands. She had a peaked cap on now, with a very shiny black bill.

"I've transferred the soup to a jar and put it in the fridge," she declared. "I have to go, Grandma. Can't be late. You sure you're okay?"

"I'm feeling fine, Sheree," said Mrs. Benison. "So much better I could even perhaps accompany you."

"The doctor did say complete rest," said Sheree.

"That was Friday," replied Mrs. Benison. She stood up from her chair very easily, and held her arms up like a sprinter crossing the finishing line in a race. Kim had never seen her move so easily before. "See, I'm vastly improved. But I know there's no time now. Make sure lots of photos get taken, so I can look at them later."

"I will," replied Sheree. "Good to meet you, Kim. Thank you again."

She turned and dashed out before Kim could say anything.

"Sheree is being given a medal today," Mrs. Benison boasted. "Presented by the governor-general."

"Congratulations," mumbled Kim. He was still thinking about Eila coming up the mountain in the dark for a nonexistent astronomy club outing and Mrs. Benison being so much better.

"When my sister came up here," he asked, "did she have a ball with her? An old basketball?"

Mrs. Benison sat down again without struggling, then frowned. Her usually sharp eyes became unfocused.

"Hmmm, yes, I do have a vague recollection. Not a basketball. Something brighter, oh so bright . . ."

Her voice trailed off. She blinked quickly and was once again her normal self.

"Would you like to borrow some books, Kim? I'm sure you'd take good care of them."

"Yes," said Kim. "Yes, please! But about that ball—"

"Any book," continued Mrs. Benison, as if Kim hadn't spoken.

"The ball Eila had with her—"

"I can recommend some books to you, if you like."

Kim hesitated. Aster—and Eila—had clearly made Mrs. Benison forget most of what had happened last night.

"I'd love to borrow a book or two. But I have to run home now. I'm late."

"Any time," said Mrs. Benison. "You and Eila are welcome any time."

Kim nodded, almost bowing over the thermos he clutched to his chest, turned around, and hurried down the hall and out, immediately heading for the downward path.

He had to find out what Eila and Aster had done.

CHAPTER FOURTEEN

Eila was in her room, reading. She looked up calmly as Kim burst in. He stopped, panting, and looked around. Aster was nowhere to be seen, but was probably under the bed. He was well aware she could roll out and zap him at any moment, so he stayed near the door.

"What did you do to Mrs. Benison?" he asked breathlessly. Blood was trickling down from his left elbow and his shorts were ripped on the side, both from being sideswiped by a branch on the way down from the mountaintop.

"We healed her," said Eila proudly. She held out her hand, and the globe slowly rolled out from under the bed, still disguised as a basketball. "Aster and I."

"You could have killed her!" snapped Kim. He kept one eye on the globe, ready to jump back. "Like that kangaroo!"

It was all too easy for him to imagine Mrs. Benison collapsed into a pile of skin and flesh, all bones removed, a horrifying lump occupying the leather armchair in her library.

"She is very old," said Eila. "If it hadn't worked, she was

going to die, anyway. Now she'll live longer, without all the pain—"

"But, Eila, you might have actually killed her! A person! A kangaroo is bad enough, but you can't risk a person's life!"

"We healed her," repeated Eila stubbornly.

"And you made her forget what happened!"

"It was necessary," said Eila. "To protect Aster. Adults mustn't know about her."

"But you interfered with her *mind!*"

"*We healed her.* That's the important thing."

Kim was silent for almost a minute. Clearly, Eila didn't or couldn't understand.

"Have you done anything to other people?" he asked finally.

"We've healed people," answered Eila, evasively.

"Who? And did you ask them first?"

"No, we didn't!" shouted Eila. "We healed people who needed to be healed!"

Eila hardly ever got angry. But she was angry now. Kim suddenly felt small and stupid, like he'd been getting it wrong all along. Eila was so certain she was doing the right thing. And Mrs. Benison *was* better . . .

Kim stopped himself. "I don't think you should be doing

things to people if they don't know about it," he said. "Even if it is healing. After all, you're only ten—"

"And you're only twelve," snapped Eila. "And everyone knows you're nowhere near as smart as me!"

Kim took a sharp intake of breath. Eila might have thought this all the time, but she'd never come out and said it before.

"I know I'm not," he said, rather shakily. "But I do have common sense, and sometimes that's more important."

"Is it?" asked Eila. "We're doing good things. Leave me and Aster alone!"

She stepped forward, and without really meaning to, Kim retreated far enough so she could slam the door. Almost in his face.

"Eila," Kim said, outside the door. But she didn't respond.

He walked away slowly, still thinking, besieged by uncertainty. Should he try to do something? But what? There was still nothing he could do about Aster. She was effectively invulnerable. Should he tell someone? No adult would believe him. Bennie had made her thoughts clear—

Bennie . . . D&D . . . Kim hurried into the kitchen and looked at the clock. It was already a few minutes past eleven. He was late for the game!

He dashed into his room, grabbed the rule books and

notes, stuffed them in his backpack, and ran outside to the shed and his waiting bike.

Before he even got to Bennie's house, he saw his friends were out in front of the garage. Madir was there too, close to Bennie's side. They all looked a bit apprehensive. Not exactly frightened, but as if they weren't sure what was happening.

"What's going on?" asked Kim as he rode up.

"My parents are having a planning session to work out how to change their jobs so they can spend more time with each other, and with us," said Bennie. She spoke slowly, as if the words were being dragged out of her. She was staring at the ground and didn't look up. "As a family."

"What?"

"Among other things, they suddenly realized we've never had a summer holiday all together," continued Bennie. "They're canceling all their work trips and making plans for us *all* to go to our grandparents'."

"For the whole summer," piped up Madir, with a bright smile. It suddenly occurred to Kim that he couldn't remember Madir ever smiling so widely before.

"Really?"

"Yeah," said Bennie. She seemed kind of dazed. She finally looked up, deliberately meeting everyone's gaze. "And they've stopped arguing. Completely."

"Dad bought Mum flowers" said Madir excitedly. "And so did Mum, but even more than he did, so he went out again and got more."

"The house is full of flowers," said Bennie disgustedly. "And they keep kissing each other!"

"It's a good change though," offered Theo. "Isn't it? I mean, it's better than them arguing, isn't it?"

"If it lasts," said Bennie.

"It will last," said Madir. She looked at Kim in a challenging way and added, "Aster."

Kim and Bennie stared at the younger girl.

"You mean Eila and Aster *made* them—" Kim started to ask.

"Yes!" exclaimed Madir. "And that proves she's good and you're wrong!"

"Who is this Aster?" asked Tamara.

"What are you talking about?" asked Theo.

Before anyone could answer, Doug Chance came out of the house, carrying a tray of iced soft drinks. Professionally, like a waiter, with only one hand under the tray.

"Hey, kids," he said, with a smile and a friendly wave. He put the tray down carefully next to Bennie. "Good to see you. We thought you might need some refreshments."

He was tall and good-looking and his teeth were super

white. Kim and the others stared at him. He'd never been so friendly before. On the rare occasions they saw him, he was always in a rush and never really acknowledged their existence.

They'd also never seen him wearing anything but a suit and tie, but today he was in white athletic shorts and shirt, with long white socks drawn up to the knee and rubber-soled tennis shoes as white as his teeth.

"Your mother and I are going to play tennis," he said to Bennie. "But we'll be back for family dinner at six. I'm going to barbecue up a feast!"

"Uh, right," stammered Bennie. Her parents did play tennis, but never together. They also never ate at a set time, and very rarely as a family. "Dinner at . . . at . . . six."

Madir kept smiling.

Doug waved again and went back into the house, calling out, "You ready, darling?"

"He *is* different," said Theo quietly.

"Yeah," agreed Kim.

"So who is Aster?" repeated Tamara. She could be very stubborn.

"Let's talk inside," said Bennie.

"I don't know," said Kim. "It might not be safe. For Theo and Tamara, I mean."

"Now I really want to know what you're talking about," said Theo.

"I don't think they'll be in any more danger if they know what's going on," said Bennie.

"There is no danger," Madir assured everyone. "Eila and Aster just want to help!"

Everyone looked at Kim.

"So, again, who is Aster?" asked Tamara.

"All right," said Kim. "I don't know ... Maybe you can help work out what we should do."

He got up and walked into the garage. The others followed and Bennie closed the door behind herself.

"You tell them," she said to Kim. "From the beginning, when we found the cut-off head."

CHAPTER FIFTEEN

"I don't believe it," said Theo.

"What part?" asked Kim.

"All of it!" exclaimed Theo. "Why are you doing this? Isn't playing D and D enough? You have to try to make us believe impossible things in real life?"

"It's all true!" spluttered Kim.

"It is," said Bennie, somberly.

"Eila found an alien globe and she's working with it to heal people?" asked Tamara. She didn't sound convinced either.

"And doing other things," said Kim. "The cloud, and who knows what else?"

"I don't believe it," repeated Theo.

"It's true," whispered Madir, who as per usual was sitting near, but not with, the group. "Aster has saved us."

She started to cry. Bennie leaped up and went to hug her.

"It's okay, Mad," she soothed. "It will be okay."

"That's what you always say!" sobbed Madir. "But it wasn't okay and it wasn't going to be okay. Mum and Dad have been going away for longer and longer! Never together! And never with us! And when they were home they argued *all the time*! If it wasn't for Eila and Aster . . ."

Her sobbing increased, her words lost.

"I'm not sure how changing your parents' behavior counts as healing," said Theo. He hastily added, "Not that I believe any of this."

Tamara took her glasses off, and started cleaning them with the hem of her tie-dyed shirt. This was a sure sign of her thinking hard about something; they all knew the telltale behavior.

"I don't know if this has anything to do with Aster," said Bennie. "They've patched things up before. I guess never like this with the flowers and the kissing, but . . ."

"It's more mind control than healing, I reckon," said Theo. "So this globe can do that, and healing—and I guess the opposite, causing harm like turning those kangaroo bones to mush, and electric shocks. It can move around by itself, and make itself heavy or light, and change its appearance. That's all? No flying?"

"Not as far as we know," said Kim. It freaked him out as much to have Theo believe him as it had to have him disbelieving.

"Why are you doing this?" burst out Tamara. She put her

glasses back on and glared at Bennie. "Making this up? Making poor Madir believe that some magic alien has fixed your parents' problems?"

"We're not—" said Kim.

"We have to show them," interrupted Bennie. "Let's go to your place, Kim."

"They'll just see a basketball," said Kim.

"Convenient for your story," said Tamara.

"They won't just see a basketball," Bennie insisted. "Not if we let the sun in."

Madir jerked away, pushing against her sister.

"No! Aster doesn't like the sun! You can't do that after she's helped us!"

"I'd like to see the basketball," said Theo.

"No!" shrieked Madir.

"Maybe we should just leave Aster alone," said Kim uneasily. "I mean, I know I wanted to get rid of her, but that doesn't seem possible, and you know, Mrs. Benison is better, and now your parents . . ."

"You're backtracking," said Tamara. "I knew it was all made up."

"No, it *isn't*," Bennie insisted. "Aster's real enough. I don't know if she's done anything to my parents, but she is real. Come on, Kim. Let's show them."

"No!" Madir protested again, trying to block the door with her small body.

"Take it easy, Mad. Aster will stop us, anyway. Nothing will happen to her. But Theo and Tamara will see we're telling the truth."

"Oh," replied Madir, calming. "Of course she will."

"Bennie, we don't need to do this." Kim remembered the electric shock all too well and he was afraid of what else Aster might do. "It doesn't matter if Theo and Tamara don't believe us. Let's just leave Aster alone, like you said before."

"I don't like being called a liar," said Bennie, her eyes narrow.

"And I don't like being lied to," said Tamara, glaring back.

"If it can be proved one way or the other, we should test it," Theo said.

"What about D and D?" asked Kim.

"We can come back and play," said Bennie.

"It's a bad idea," repeated Kim.

But everyone else was getting up and heading out. Kim followed, feeling sick. He felt even worse when he saw Bennie's parents in their convertible in the street. It was running, but still parked—they weren't in any hurry to go anywhere. They were so busy talking about how lovely the flowers they'd given each other were, interspersing their praises with kisses, that they didn't even notice the kids pick up their bikes and ride away.

It has be mind control, thought Kim.

They rode up the hill in a gaggle. As per usual, there was almost no traffic; they only had to go into single file once. The car that passed was driven by one of the scientists who often came to the experimental farm; she beeped her horn as she went past, with a friendly wave out the window.

"Don't tell my parents about D and D," Kim reminded Theo and Tamara as they approached the gates. "We've been playing table tennis, okay? Hopefully we won't see them anyway."

"Have they seen this magic globe?" asked Theo.

"Dad saw a basketball," replied Kim. "Quiet now."

They rode into the shed and put their bikes down, and silently went into the house. Just as they got to Eila's door, Madir tried to dash to the front of the group, but Bennie held her back.

Kim knocked and opened the door immediately. Everyone rushed in.

Eila was at her desk, books open in front of her. The only light came from her reading lamp. The curtains were drawn tightly together, with several heavy books leaned against them to keep them closed.

"What do you all want?" asked Eila. "I thought you were playing your stupid game."

"They want to see Aster," croaked Kim.

Bennie let Madir go and edged around closer to the window.

"I don't know what you're talking about," said Eila.

"We've told them," continued Kim.

"You have to stop making things up, Kim."

"I knew it," said Tamara.

Kim gulped and knelt down. He saw Aster immediately, and the single red dot opening and closing like an evil wink.

"She's under the bed," he said.

Tamara knelt down too.

"It's just an old basketball," she said. "Like the ones at school."

"Get it out, then," said Kim, standing up. His voice had gone weirdly husky. He shifted his weight, instinctively ready to run.

Tamara got down on her stomach, reached under the bed, and pulled out the basketball. She stood up with it and held it out to Theo, who tapped his knuckles on the ball.

"Might need to be pumped up a bit," he said, clearly disappointed.

Bennie lunged at the curtains and snatched back one

side, sending books tumbling. A shaft of sunlight beamed across the room, narrowly missing Tamara and the globe.

Aster reacted immediately. A bolt of blinding blue electricity shot through the air, sending Bennie hurtling back against the wall. The globe leaped out of Tamara's grasp onto the bed and rolled into the darkest corner. Most of its basketball camouflage disappeared, patches of fake orange rippling over the golden light now revealed beneath.

Eila was quick, too, jumping up to pull the curtain back in place.

Kim rushed over to Bennie, who was collapsed in the corner, her head on her drawn-up knees. He lifted her chin to look at her face. Her eyes were closed, her mouth slack, her head lolled without support.

"You've killed her," he cried out. "You've killed her!"

CHAPTER SIXTEEN

"She isn't dead," said Eila in her superior voice. "Aster doesn't kill."

Despite saying this, she knelt down next to Kim and put her palm on Bennie's forehead. The room grew brighter as Aster suddenly shone with greater intensity, the basketball disguise completely gone. Eila's hand glowed too, with the same brilliant light.

Madir edged close to Eila, biting her knuckles and looking down at Bennie, clearly torn between her loyalty to her friend and her fear for her sister.

"She's fine," concluded Eila, withdrawing her hand. The light around her fingers faded away. "Knocked out. She'll come to in a minute or so."

Kim leaned back and wiped his eyes with his hands. Madir stopped biting her knuckles.

"I'm sorry I didn't believe you," said Theo. His voice was shaky.

"Me too," whispered Tamara. She had retreated to the doorway.

"There's no need to be afraid," said Eila. She sounded

like a teacher addressing a class, not a ten-year-old talking to twelve-year-olds. "Aster only acts in self-defense. Bennie knows that, she brought this on herself."

Bennie groaned and sat up a bit.

"What happened?" she mumbled.

"Aster zapped you," said Kim. "You were right about the sunshine."

"Why does it . . . *she* avoid sunlight?" Theo asked Eila.

"You don't need to know," Eila replied. "I've told Kim that a million times, and I'm getting sick of it. Aster is simply here to learn and she is also helping me do some good things. You have to leave both of us alone so we can keep doing what we need to do without being interrupted by a bunch of scared kids."

'Where's she from? What does she want?" continued Theo.

"You. Don't. Need. To. Know," said Eila. "Please leave."

Tamara needed no encouraging. She turned and hurried out. Kim helped Bennie up, and then with Theo's help, they all left. Madir hesitated but stayed behind.

Eila shut the door firmly after the twelve-year-olds.

"My room," said Kim. They hustled over to it, went in, and laid Bennie down on the bed. But soon she sat up again, massaging her temples.

"Wow," she said. "That was almost as bad as when I got hit in the head with the softball bat. Remember, Patty Keen was practicing her swing and just let it go?"

"I remember, yeah, for sure," chorused Kim, Theo, and Tamara.

"Almost, but not as bad," said Bennie. "So, you got something to say, Tamara?"

"I already said sorry I didn't believe you," replied Tamara. She was cleaning her glasses again. "Only you were unconscious."

"I said sorry too," Theo chimed in.

"Hey, do you think Aster could fix my eyes?" asked Tamara.

"Maybe," said Kim. "Or maybe she'd make you go blind. I think the 'healing' is pretty risky. Eila said Aster thought it was worth the risk with Mrs. Benison because she's close to dying, anyway."

Tamara put her glasses back on.

"So she could have killed my parents?" asked Bennie. She sounded strangely unemotional about the possibility.

"I don't know," said Kim. "Aster did kill the kangaroo and the guinea pigs."

"So she *does* kill," said Theo. "Eila lied about that."

"Well, killing by accident while trying to do something

isn't the same as killing on purpose," pointed out Tamara. "And they were animals, not people."

"I wonder why this Aster is doing what Eila wants," said Theo. "And whether she'll keep doing that."

"Eila thinks she will," said Kim.

"Yeah, well, Eila is ten," said Theo. "Even if she is super smart. What if Aster is only going along with her for now? She must have her own plans."

"Not every alien wants to take over the world," said Tamara.

"How do we know?" asked Theo. "I mean, this is the first alien we know is for real."

"*If* Aster is an alien," Kim pointed out. "She could be something else. Magic. Supernatural. We just don't know."

"Whatever it is, we should tell someone," said Tamara. "The police, our parents, or someone else from the government."

"They'd just see a basketball," said Kim with a sigh. "And if we tried to let the sun in again, Aster might zap everyone and who knows what else."

"We've already talked about all this," said Bennie. She got off the bed and straightened up, testing her balance. "Kim and me, I mean. There's nothing we can do, and so far Eila has been right—they're only healing people and doing good things, give or take some ants and a few animals. So let's forget about it and go and play D and D."

"There might be something we can do," said Theo. "We should keep thinking about it, make plans."

"Why?" asked Tamara.

"Just in case," said Theo. "What if Aster does turn out to want to take over the world? We'll have to stop her."

"Yeah, but how?" asked Bennie.

"That's why we have to keep thinking," said Theo. "Observe. Plan. Act. That's what I do in D and D. As Altmoor."

"But we don't have any spells," Kim pointed out. "Or magic weapons. Or anything."

"We've got our brains," said Theo.

"So we watch and wait," said Bennie. "And try to think up a plan. That's it?"

"Yeah," said Theo. "A contingency plan."

"A what?" asked Kim.

"That's the kind of plan you have in case something happens, but you hope you don't have to use. Like being prepared for an emergency. So we make a contingency plan for what to do if Aster turns out to be an evil alien who wants to take over the planet. But we hope we don't have to use it."

"How is that different from just hoping nothing bad happens?" Tamara challenged.

"It is different, because we'll have a plan," said Theo.

"Like what?" asked Kim.

"I don't know yet," replied Theo patiently. "Like I said: We have to observe Eila and Aster, see what they do."

"Yeah, maybe we'll spot a weakness, like you said before Kim," added Bennie.

"We've already seen one," said Tamara suddenly. "Sunshine."

Theo shook his head. "It's an unknown. We don't know if it's a weakness. Maybe Aster avoids the sunlight because it will make her angry or something, and she doesn't want to go berserk."

"I didn't think of that," said Bennie. "Geez! Imagine if I'd made things worse . . ."

"It was just an idea," Tamara muttered.

"It's worth thinking about," said Theo. "But we need to know. Maybe you can learn more about Aster from Eila, Kim?"

"She's hardly talking to me," said Kim dolefully. "And she won't answer my questions."

"You'll have to watch her, see where she goes with Aster."

"But it's always at night! I might not wake up."

"You just have to try."

"It's all right for you to say that."

"Mad might know something," said Bennie. "I'll ask her when she's sleepy, tonight."

"See, the plan's already coming together!" exclaimed Theo.

"It's not much of one," grumbled Kim. "I have to stay awake all night and Bennie questions Madir when she's sleepy! Anyone got any other ideas?"

They were all silent for almost a minute.

Finally, Bennie threw her hands up in the air.

"Come on! There's no point sitting in here trying to think up plans. Let's go back to my place and play D and D."

"Are you sure you're okay?" asked Kim.

"Yeah, it wasn't so bad, I feel fine now," said Bennie. She still looked rather pale but was standing easily enough. "Come on! D and D time!"

"Not so loud!" cautioned Kim.

Bennie nodded solemnly, and they left the house without talking any more. As they rode out, Kim looked back and saw his parents coming out of greenhouse two. He wasn't sure if they'd seen him or not, but in any case, they didn't shout to call him back.

"I want to swap out some of my old spells for new ones," said Theo as they rode. "From *Greyhawk*. Is that okay?"

"Yeah, sure," said Kim. "Remember, we finished last week with you all at the inn, The Sign of the Singed Owl, so we'll start the next morning. You can have new spells and be healed up and everything. Unless you roll a one, that'll mean something went wrong overnight."

"Like what?" asked Bennie.

"Roll a one and find out," said Kim.

"What if we roll a twenty?" asked Tamara.

"You slept really well," said Kim. "I'll give you plus one on saving throws for the morning."

"I wish I was a thaumaturgist and could get Fireball," said Theo.

"What level is thaumaturgist?" asked Bennie.

"Five," answered Theo. "And there's Lightning Bolt too. That would be handy."

"You going to use any of the new monsters, Kim?" asked Tamara.

"What about the magic items?" asked Bennie.

"You'll see," said Kim. "The Town Wizard has called you in again, by the way. She's got a job for you. She wants something brought back from a dungeon under the Al-Greza pyramid, some fifty leagues from Opir . . ."

CHAPTER SEVENTEEN

Through the next week, Kim did his best to be sure he'd wake up if Eila and Aster went out. The first thing he did was stick three drawing pins on the top of Eila's bedroom door so it would make a slight grating noise when it opened or shut. That was nerve-racking enough—he had to do it super fast during dinner while pretending he'd gone to the toilet, and he had to stand on a chair and hope Aster wouldn't notice or stop him. But he managed it, and was rewarded with the sound of the door scraping later when Eila went to bed.

He also tried to stay awake later than usual. Not secretly reading in his wardrobe, but sitting by his own door with it slightly ajar, listening. This was boring and tiring, and he kept nodding off.

But Eila and Aster didn't go out, he was pretty sure, and he reported this to the others at school. They had a meeting every lunchtime, under the oaks. Theo called it a "mission status report," but the first three days of the week there was nothing to report. Kim hadn't seen anything, and Bennie had failed to get any information from Madir.

Things changed on Wednesday night, an hour after the Basalts had all gone to bed. Kim was sitting with his back to the wall next to his door, trying not to nod off, when he heard the scrape of Eila's door opening. He heard her footsteps, the characteristic sound of her loose sole, which he still hadn't mended.

Then they stopped. He didn't hear the front door. Or the kitchen door.

Kim eased his own door open and stuck his head out, staying low.

Eila was standing in front of their parents' bedroom. She had Aster in her arms, the globe glowing with a pale, golden radiance. As he watched, the glow intensified and began to flicker, as it had done when she had been studying the ants.

Eila reached out and opened the door, and Aster's strange light grew brighter still, and flickered faster, all of it directed into Darwin and Marie's bedroom.

Kim got up and charged down the hall, not caring how noisy he was.

"Eila!" he shouted. "What are you doing?"

He was six feet away when a jolt of electricity arced

out of Aster and crackled across the floor in front of him. Kim windmilled his arms and almost fell as he slid to a halt.

"Don't come any closer, Kim," warned Eila out of the corner of her mouth. She didn't turn her head, all her focus ahead. "This is difficult and if you interrupt us, Mum and Dad might get hurt. Stay still and keep *quiet*."

Kim opened his mouth, then shut it. He wanted to lunge forward and try to smack the globe out of Eila's arms, but he knew he couldn't do it before he was electrocuted. He might have tried though if it wasn't for the threat to his parents.

He stood still, his heart racing even more than when he finished the school cross-country championship, which he'd won the last two years in a row. Bennie tended to beat him in all the athletics competitions, and she was a faster sprinter, but Kim could run long distances.

But he felt far worse now than at the end of any long-distance run. All he could do was stand there, clutching his chest and panting, waiting for the worst.

Finally, after what seemed a really long time but was probably only minutes, Aster's flickering light slowed, and the globe dulled. Eila turned to Kim.

"What have you done to Mum and Dad?" he asked his

sister. He could hardly speak, terror rising up to make his voice and every part of him tremble.

"We haven't *done* anything to them," replied Eila stiffly. "Only a minor adjustment to something they were both thinking about, anyway. They're fine. They're in a deep sleep now and will wake up feeling great."

"You've interfered with their brains!" shouted Kim. Anger helped him overcome the fear. "You've used mind control on them!"

"We've encouraged something that was already there," said Eila.

"*We?*" snapped Kim. "You mean *I*. Eila, you can't do this. They're our parents! Imagine if someone was messing with your mind."

"They won't know," said Eila defensively. "It's a very small thing."

"What if it had gone wrong? Oh, why are we even talking about this! You're mind controlling our parents!"

Eila face grew expressionless, her posture stiffer.

"I'm only doing what needs to be done," she said. "I made Bennie's parents see what they were doing to each other and their kids, didn't I? And change for the better? Madir hardly ever saw them, and when she did, they were arguing with each other. Always! She thought it might somehow be her fault!"

Kim shook his head. "But . . . but that doesn't mean you should—"

"And I healed Mrs. Benison," said Eila. "As much as possible. She was in constant pain. I heard Mum say some days she could hardly move from rheumatism."

"But you didn't ask them," protested Kim. "I mean, yes, you've done good things. But why not ask them first?"

"Adults must not know about Aster," said Eila. She said it like it was a law, or a golden rule.

"And what *have* you done to Mum and Dad?"

"I told you. I simply encouraged them to do something they were thinking about, anyway. That's all. You'll see."

"Where are you going to stop, Eila?" asked Kim. "Are you going to make them let you off your chores? Or stay home from school? You've started controlling them now. What's next?"

Eila frowned.

"I'm not going to do anything else to Mum and Dad," she said. "This is just . . . the once. Aster needs something and—

"Aster has turned you into a monster," said Kim, and to his own horror, started crying. Tears spilled down his cheeks, and there was nothing he could do to stop them.

He couldn't stop crying. He couldn't stop Aster. He couldn't do anything. He turned away and stumbled back to his own room, shaking and shivering as if struck by a sudden fever.

A minute later, he heard the scrape and thud of Eila's door closing.

CHAPTER EIGHTEEN

"So what is Eila getting your parents to do?" asked Theo.

The mood of the lunchtime mission report was down. Kim had struggled to tell them what had happened, and Bennie had stiffened up and looked dangerous when he mentioned what Eila had said about her parents' arguing and Madir thinking it was her fault.

"I don't know," said Kim. He shrugged. "They did seem fine this morning. Everything was normal. We had breakfast, they went out to do their jobs. I came to school."

"You get anything out of Madir?" Tamara asked Bennie, who was trying to run up the closest tree to grab a low branch. "And you'll never get up the tree that way."

"Says you." Panting, Bennie managed to get halfway up before falling back. "Madir won't talk. She knows what I'm trying to do, so she doesn't talk at all when she goes to bed. She won't even say good night."

"Maybe we should try the sunlamp thing," said Kim. He stood up and ran at the same tree Bennie had attempted, but only managed to bounce off and fall on the ground. He groaned and lay back on the grass, spreading his arms wide. "I want to do something!"

"We need more information," said Theo.

"You can't run up a tree like that," said Tamara to Bennie.

"You can't run up trees full stop," said Kim. "No one can."

"I saw a guy do it in a movie," Bennie insisted. She tried again, and actually made two or three steps up the trunk before falling back.

"Maybe it was a different kind of tree," said Theo.

"Yeah, I think the bark needs to be more . . . more grippy," said Bennie. She flopped down next to Kim.

"So what about the sunlamps?" Kim spoke to the sky, not getting up. "How many can you get from your mum's shop, Tam?"

"It's a pharmacy, not a shop," said Tamara. "Mum says we always have to correct anyone who says it's a shop. And she's a pharmacist, not a chemist."

"Okay, how many sunlamps can you borrow from the pharmacy?" asked Kim.

"I think there's about five in the stockroom out the back."

"These are the sort you plug in, right?" asked Theo. "Not battery operated?"

"Yes," replied Tamara.

"Pretty hard to deploy them," said Theo. Both Theo's

parents were in the Army, so he often used words like *deploy*.

"You mean *use them*," said Bennie.

"We'd have to get Eila and Aster to come somewhere we had them set up, all ready to flick on," said Kim. He sat up, interested now. "Your garage, Bennie. If we had a lamp in each corner, maybe she couldn't electrocute us all at the same time."

"That's a big maybe," said Theo. "For all we know, Aster can control electricity, so the lamps wouldn't turn on. And like I said, we don't know what sunshine will do to her."

"We have to try *something*," said Kim.

Theo made a fake throat-clearing noise.

"What?" asked Tamara. "You got an idea?"

"The weak point is Eila," said Theo.

Silence greeted this sally.

"What do you mean?" asked Kim.

"If Eila controls what Aster does, then whoever controls Eila controls Aster," said Theo smugly. "It's logical."

"So what are you suggesting?" asked Kim.

"I'm not suggesting anything, I'm just pointing out—"

"We could kidnap Eila," said Bennie. "Hide her up the mountain. You know, that fallen-down shack . . ."

"We're not kidnapping Eila," said Kim. "She's my sister, remember?"

"She's in league with a supernatural *thing*," said Theo.

"A mostly friendly one," said Tamara quietly.

"Kidnapping Eila would be a waste of time," added Kim. "She still wouldn't do anything we asked. And besides, I think she can talk to Aster telepathically. Mind to mind. So she'd just tell her where she was and come nighttime the globe would roll up and zap everybody."

"What if . . . what if . . . uh . . . no," said Theo.

"What?" asked Bennie.

"Nothing," said Theo. "I was thinking too much like it's a game. Not real life."

"What?" repeated Bennie.

"Well, I was thinking . . . It's wrong, I know, just a thought . . . but we could kill Eila—"

"What?!" shouted Kim. "No!"

"I already said it wasn't a real idea," protested Theo. "Besides, maybe it would make everything worse. I mean, if Eila is holding Aster back from whatever she really wants to do."

"No killing, no kidnapping—that's final," said Kim.

"Any other ideas?" asked Bennie.

No one offered any.

"Meeting over, then," said Theo. "Kim keeps watching. We keep thinking."

"Maybe Tamara should get the sunlamps, in case," said Kim thoughtfully.

Tamara shook her head. "I'm not taking the lamps unless we have a good reason. Mum'll notice if they're gone for more than a day or two. And we'll have to be careful not to break them and keep the boxes all good and everything."

"What if the whole future of the world is at stake?" asked Theo.

"Well, it isn't, so far," said Tamara. She hesitated, then said, "I asked Eila about fixing my eyesight, by the way."

"What?" spat Kim.

"She said she can't do eyes yet," said Tamara defensively. "They're too complicated. Only what she called persuasion—"

"Mind control," interrupted Kim.

"I'm just telling you what she said. And bones and joints and so on, like for Mrs. Benison."

"You'd better not be going over to the enemy, Tam," said Theo.

"Are they the enemy though?" asked Tamara. "I don't mind your 'contingency' planning, Theo, but I don't think we should do anything unless there's a really good reason."

"Mind controlling my parents isn't enough?" asked Kim.

"Depends on what she got them to do," said Tamara.

"Yeah, I'm dying to know what it is," said Bennie. "I mean, she could have got them to do anything! Uh, sorry, Kim. I know it's bad. Only . . ."

"Yeah, I know," said Kim wearily. "How are your parents?"

"Weird," said Bennie, with a puzzled frown. "I mean, they're not arguing. They want to know about what I'm doing at school! They both helped Mad with her homework last night. They wanted to help me too . . ."

Her voice trailed off, the frown deepening, before she changed the subject.

"Hey, maybe Aster's got your parents to give you less work. You won't have to chip bricks any more!"

"I don't mind chipping bricks," said Kim. "I just want them to be the same as they always are. I hate waiting to find out what Aster's done. What *Eila's* done."

The bell rang for the end of lunch. Kim's voice trailed off. They started walking back, before first Bennie and then Theo started to run, and then they were all running back across the oval, lost in the mindlessness of sudden exercise.

CHAPTER NINETEEN

What Eila and Aster had done to the Basalt parents was immediately clear when Kim got home. There was a brand-new color television set in the living room.

Kim stared at it. There was a note on top of the set. He walked across to read it, and saw his mother's handwriting.

"'Not to be turned on without express permission,'" he read aloud, strangely relieved. While this was clearly the result of Aster's "persuasion," his parents were still making strict rules.

He was so relieved he voluntarily went and chipped bricks for an hour, increasing his total by twenty-three, which did absolutely nothing to reduce the size of the unchipped brick stack.

The new television was the first topic of conversation at dinner.

"Your grandmother gave us the money for a television set a few years ago," said Darwin. "But we thought you both too young and television too intrusive to buy one back then. However, we realize television can be useful, so we decided it was time."

"But it will go away again if our rules are not followed," said Marie. "You can only watch programs we approve in advance, and no more than four hours per week."

"That sounds sensible," said Eila. She ignored Kim's glare. "Television can be an important educational resource."

"What if we don't want to watch it at all?" asked Kim.

"Then don't," said Darwin. "But I am surprised. You've asked us to get a television many times, Kim. What's changed?"

"I . . . I changed my mind," said Kim weakly. He glared at Eila again, but she ignored him.

"What about the show you always pester me about?" asked Darwin. "*Doctor Who*? You told me science fiction has a lot of science in it. Surely you want to watch that?"

"I'm not sure when it's on," muttered Kim, who knew very well when *Doctor Who* was on because all his friends watched it and told him about it until he asked them to shut up as he had no chance of ever seeing it.

"There's a television guide in the newspaper," said Darwin. "Every Monday. We might have this week's, come to think of it. I haven't lined any beds this week. See if you can find it after dinner, Kim."

Kim nodded. His father seemed quite interested in

watching television himself, he noted. More than his mother.

The visiting scientists brought their newspapers from homes, offices, and labs after they'd read them, and after Marie and Darwin had read them too, they were put in the shed, for later use in lining the bottom of garden beds.

There were a lot of newspapers stacked up in the shed. Kim started to sort through them to find the previous Monday's. It was near the top, and the first thing he saw was a picture on the front page of Chief Inspector Benison. He scanned the article beneath it. It was all about her getting the medal Mrs. Benison had mentioned. It was for bravery. She'd saved a group of tourists from a crocodile, after they'd been picnicking somewhere they shouldn't have been. Inspector Benison had shot the crocodile through the eye at the last minute as it charged up the beach—it had almost gotten her. The article said she was a champion shot, and had won a silver medal at the Mexico City Olympic games seven years ago.

Kim was puzzled about a saltwater crocodile being in the lake, until he read the part about Inspector Benison having been stationed in the Northern Territory; she'd only come back to the city this year. So the crocodile was up there. They had sharks as well, he knew, and sometimes the sharks and crocodiles fought each other. He made a mental note to tell Bennie about Sheree Benison standing her ground to shoot a crocodile through the eye at the last minute, and continued his search.

He found the television guide almost immediately afterward, in that same issue. It was printed on pink paper as an insert. He scanned it on the way back inside. There seemed little point in not watching television now that they had one. His parents wouldn't even know he wasn't watching as a protest against Eila and Aster. But as he already knew, *Doctor Who* was on at six p.m., the Basalt family dinner time. Maybe there was something else . . .

Eila was washing up when he came back in from the shed with the guide. Kim heard the television from the living room, a woman newsreader speaking in a very clear voice about something to do with banks and inflation.

"They're watching the news," said Eila. "We're not allowed. Or maybe you are."

Kim put the TV guide on the table and started drying the cutlery. It felt weird doing something so ordinary when there was so much tension between them.

And Aster was only twenty feet away, lurking under Eila's bed.

They worked in silence for some time. Kim was up to drying the last few plates before he spoke.

"Can Aster hear whatever I say to you?"

"Not unless I want her to," replied Eila, pulling the plug on the sink. "Why would she want to hear what you have to say?"

"I don't know," mumbled Kim. "Why did she want us to get a television?"

"To learn more. She can watch everything that's on if there's a set nearby," said Eila. "Both channels at the same time."

"You haven't done any more mind control, have you?" asked Kim nervously.

"No." Eila turned to Kim and looked him in the eye. "But we will if I think it needs to be done."

"Could you mind control me?" asked Kim. "Make me forget about Aster, for example?"

As soon as he said it, he saw realization dawn on Eila's face. She hadn't thought of making him forget, he saw, and he wished he hadn't given her the idea. But it was too late.

"I don't know," she answered, a second too slow. "You resisted her, in the lake."

"Well, don't try!" said Kim.

"Try what?" asked Marie, walking into the room. "Have you wiped the table, Kim?"

"Uh, nothing," said Kim. He grabbed the Wettex, wrung it quickly, and started wiping the table. Eila dried the last plate and put it away. Marie watched them for a moment, then went out the back door to check the watering systems, as she or Darwin did every night before going to bed.

She has no idea what Eila and Aster have done, Kim thought.

And now he had to fear he'd be next.

Kim sat with his back to the bedroom door when he notionally went to bed. He put his shoes back on after he got changed into his pajamas, to be ready for anything, even though he hoped nothing would happen. He cursed himself for suggesting to Eila that she could make him forget about Aster. He imagined the globe rolling down the hallway, coming into his room . . . that fast-flickering light, and the cold tendrils reaching into his brain . . .

There was a noise outside. The soft *snick-snick* of Eila's door opening and shutting. Kim started and pushed back harder against the door, flexing his knees, holding it shut. He waited to hear Eila's footsteps, that loose slipper flop, coming closer and closer . . .

But he didn't hear any footsteps. Kim frowned and

turned to put his ear against the door. He could hear something, very faintly. The snick of a door closing—the back door.

Eila and Aster were going out. *Eila must have put on her sneakers*, thought Kim. That's why he hadn't heard her.

He hesitated. He'd told the others he would watch. They needed to know what Eila and Aster were up to. But he was even more fearful than he had been before.

He took a deep breath and got to his feet. Creeping out, he kept close to the walls, trying to be unobtrusive. He hesitated again by the back door, but finally opened it a crack and peered out.

There was no one there. Kim went out and around the side of the house, pausing to listen every few steps. But all he could hear were the usual noises of the night. He looked around, squinting in the darkness, but there were only the streetlights down the hill, the distant government lab floodlights, and the stars above.

He crossed the lawn and stopped, looked around again, and listened. He was about to give up and go back in when he saw a faint glow moving beyond the front gate. It was low to the ground, about as bright as a candle, without the flickering.

Kim knew what it was immediately.

Aster was rolling along by herself, not being carried by Eila, who was presumably walking behind. He was pretty sure they were heading for the path up the mountain.

Kim hesitated again, fighting back an urgent desire to run inside, jump into bed, and put his head under the pillow. But he thought about what Bennie in particular would say if he did that. So he clenched his fists, took several fast breaths, and followed.

Whatever Eila and Aster were doing, he would find out.

CHAPTER TWENTY

Climbing up the mountain path in the dark was not easy. Kim was surprised that Eila and Aster were managing to go so quickly, though Eila would have some benefit from the globe's dim light. He kept running into unseen branches, and almost twisted his ankle in a hole that remained invisible even after he put his foot in it.

By the time he got to Mrs. Benison's house, his face was scratched, his ankle hurt, and he was sweaty and sort of cold—a bad combination. He stopped at the edge of the trees, kneeling down to look ahead. There were lights on in the house, spilling out through the windows to partially illuminate the lawn.

Kim half choked on his own spit in surprise, as he saw Aster rolling across Mrs. Benison's lawn.

Eila wasn't with her.

The globe was alone.

He watched as Aster crossed the yellow painted lines of the future parking lot and rolled on up to the road, turning right to continue to the summit and the television mast. When she was about a hundred yards away, he ran across the lawn to the shadow of the house and crouched again.

Aster had reached the bottom of the mast. He could see the glow of the globe and the faint outline of the metal struts in the starlight, and the much brighter red glow atop the mast, the light warning aircraft of its presence.

"What are you doing?" he whispered to himself.

This was a mistake. Aster either actually heard him speak or detected the thought behind it, because all of a sudden a beam of light like a small searchlight shone from the base of the mast. It flickered and began to move down the mountainside, a finger of light, tapping and searching. Searching for Kim.

Still crouching, he ran around to the front of the house and crawled under the veranda. He saw the probing light quest around one side of the house, and then the other. He lay still. A few minutes later the light came back again, still searching.

Something crawled across his hand. He jerked it away, stifling a cry. It was probably a spider, a huntsman or a wolf spider. He wanted to scream "Don't bite me! Don't bite me!" but knew he had to keep silent.

The light didn't come back. Kim kept waiting, just in case, occasionally flicking his hands and feet to discourage anything that might otherwise want to crawl onto him.

He couldn't tell how much time passed, but eventually he couldn't bear it anymore. He pulled himself out from under the veranda and crawled to the side of the house.

The finger of light was gone. Kim stared up at the television mast. He was looking at the bottom of it, searching for Aster's golden glow, when he caught sight of it high up. Below the red aircraft warning light!

Aster had somehow climbed up to the top of the television mast. Kim wondered what on earth she was doing, but he didn't speak his thought aloud. He tried to hardly breathe, to make no sound at all.

I'm a kangaroo, he thought, in case Aster could detect his watchfulness. He turned it into a simple song, repeating inside his head.

I'm a kangaroo
Eating grass
Boohoo
I'm a kangaroo
Eating grass
Boohoo

He kept that going for what felt like a long time. It got colder, and he began to shiver, but he continued the mental song and didn't move.

The golden light shifted position, below the red. The song stuttered in Kim's head, but he got it going again, peering up toward the tower as he tried to work out exactly what he was seeing.

Aster was flying. Or levitating, maybe. He could see the golden dot coming down, but it was arcing away from the tower, not climbing down the ladder. The globe was on a gliding path, slowly descending toward . . . Mrs. Benison's lawn!

Kim dropped to the ground again and edged back until he could only just see around the corner of the house. Aster continued to descend, coming closer and closer, until the globe landed on the far side of the lawn, near the beginning of the path downhill.

Kim held his breath. The globe sat there for a few seconds, then began to roll away, following the path back down toward the experimental farm. He watched it till it dropped out of sight down the slope, and even then waited a few minutes more in case Aster doubled back.

But she didn't double back. The air was growing colder, and he was already cold from keeping still, and tired, and the scratches on his face were stinging. Part of the sky was clouded now, thankfully not directly above, so he felt sure it was natural. He could smell rain in the air.

Kim crossed the lawn, very slowly. At the top of the path, he peered down. He could see a very faint glow from the globe, traveling fast, rolling downhill as if Aster was just a basketball someone had thrown down the mountain.

He followed, much more slowly, shivering and trying to think. Did Eila know Aster was out by herself? Would that make any difference?

Kim was almost back at the farm when the rain came. It fell hard and fast, and within a minute, his pajamas were soaked through. He'd lost sight of Aster, and presumed she was back inside the house, so he sped up, walking faster and faster in an effort to get out of the rain.

He only noticed the kitchen light was on when he was a couple feet away from the back door. Instantly, he stopped. But it was too late; he'd been spotted through the kitchen window. His father threw the door open and bellowed, "Kim! Where have you been?"

"Uh, I heard something," said Kim, trudging inside. He stepped aside as his father closed the door, shutting out the noise of the rain and the cold air. "I went out to see what it was, but I fell over."

He gestured at the scratches on his face.

"Yeah, I heard something too," said Darwin. He was wearing a raincoat over his pajamas, and had one

Wellington boot on, the other in his hand. He peered at Kim's face, saw the scratches were minor, and leaned back on the kitchen table to put the other boot on. "You should have woken me up, Kim. Did you see anyone?"

"A light," stammered Kim. "Like a torch maybe. Going out the gate."

"Plant thieves," said Darwin. "It's been a long time since we had that kind of trouble."

Kim blinked. He didn't know they'd ever had a problem with people stealing plants.

"Have a shower and wash those scratches properly," said Darwin. "I'm going to wake up your mother, then have a look around. That broomstick you broke might come in handy."

"Uh, okay." Kim couldn't believe he was going to get away with sneaking out at night, or that his father was going out into the night with a broken broomstick to look for luckily nonexistent thieves. "Since I'm already wet, maybe I should come with you?"

"No, you go have a shower," said Darwin. He hopped around, settling his foot in the boot he'd just put on. "Get changed and go back to bed."

Kim nodded and scuttled through the kitchen, leaving wet footprints.

Eila's bedroom door was shut. Kim looked at it, thinking he might wake her up, but his father came along the hall behind him, so he hurried on into the bathroom.

He'd talk to Eila in the morning.

CHAPTER TWENTY-ONE

"Kim, there's no point making stuff like that up," said Eila. Her superior voice was fully deployed. "I *know* Aster didn't go out by herself."

"How do you think I got these scratches, then?" asked Kim, pointing at his face.

"Falling over outside looking for the plant thieves or whoever they were," said Eila.

"That's just the story I told Dad! Aster went up the television mast, Eila. And she flew back down!"

"Aster was with me all night," Eila calmly insisted. "And she can't fly. You're being ridiculous. More ridiculous than ever."

"She's up to something you don't know about," warned Kim.

"That's not possible," said Eila, with total certainty. "Can we go now, please? It's going to start raining again soon."

"You go," said Kim. "I have to lock the gate. You got your key?"

Eila nodded and pushed off, pedaling slowly.

Kim pulled the gate shut with some effort, looped the chain through, and fastened the padlock. Then he realized he'd left his bike on the inside of the fence and had to unlock the padlock, open the gate, wheel the bike through, and repeat the process.

He hoped Eila hadn't seen that, but a laugh told him she had. Sure enough, she'd stopped just down the road and was looking back.

"I'm distracted!" shouted Kim. Plus he'd never had to lock the gate before. Darwin had taken the threat of supposed plant thieves seriously and put the padlock and chain on the gate and given his children keys with the strict instruction they were not to share or lose them.

By the time he got to Bennie's, the story of the plant thieves and his embarrassment with the gate had already been relayed by Eila. Bennie stifled her laugh as Kim rode up, and Eila and Madir took off.

"Plant thieves!" she exclaimed. "I wish I'd been there to fight them off with you!"

"There weren't any plant thieves," said Kim crossly. "That's just what Dad thought, and I went along. He must have woken up when Aster went back in."

"What? So what did happen?"

Kim explained as they rode to school.

"Phew!" said Bennie. "This'll shake up the mission briefing meeting!"

It did shake up the meeting. Even Tamara, who had seemed to doubt whether any contingency plan would be needed, was convinced that they needed to try the sunlamp ambush. The news about Aster rolling around by herself was unsettling to everyone.

"So we should set the lamps up in the garage," said Bennie. "How do we get Eila and Aster down there at night?"

"You tell her your parents are arguing again," suggested Kim. "Ask for her help."

"But Madir will tell her they're fine."

Kim thought for a moment.

"If you come up at, say, quarter past seven, I reckon my parents will be watching the news, now we have the color television—"

Everyone else spoke at once, basically saying the same thing.

"You have a *color* television!"

"Oh yeah, I forgot, that was what Eila 'persuaded' them to do. Apparently my grandma wanted us to have one and gave them the money ages ago—"

"This is an important detail," said Theo. "Aster wanted a television, and she goes out at night and does something up the television mast? We needed to know both pieces of information. It's all related—"

"Well, you know it now," said Kim. "So, Bennie, you come up about quarter past seven and tell Eila you need her and Aster's help. She won't be able to check with Madir because we don't have a phone. So Eila will come down once my parents are asleep, probably around ten— that's when she often goes out. So Mad'll be in bed. You meet Eila and Aster, tell them your parents are having a big argument in the garage. We have all the sunlamps in place—"

"I can't get the lamps tonight," said Tamara. "It's late-night shopping. We're open till nine, and my mum will be there the whole time. I probably can't get them till Sunday when we're shut. I've got a key."

"Okay, so we do everything on Sunday," said Kim.

"What about D and D?" asked Bennie.

"We can still play D and D," said Kim. "We should do what we normally do anyway, so Eila doesn't get suspicious."

"I think the television mast needs to be checked out," said Theo. "To see what Aster was doing up there."

"Why do you keep calling it a mast?" asked Tamara.

"Because that's what it is," said Theo.

"It's a tower."

"No, it isn't, because it's held up with wires, you know, like a tent. And it's open inside, like Meccano."

"It doesn't matter what you call it," said Bennie. "But you're right—we should see what Aster was doing up there."

"There's probably nothing to see, maybe Aster just wanted to look at the stars or something, " said Kim, who knew what the glint in Bennie's eye meant.

"Communicating with the alien fleet," said Theo.

"We should look, this arvo," said Bennie. "We can ride our bikes up the road."

"Not my bike," said Kim. "I'd have to walk it most of the way. And like I said, we should lie low, not do anything to make Eila suspicious."

"You said Mrs. Benison offered to lend you some books," said Bennie. "We could go up to do that straight after school and look at the tower—the mast—as well. That's not suspicious. Who's coming?"

Her question led to several minutes of hearty disagreement. Even Theo, who thought the mast needed to be investigated, didn't want to ride up the mountain, and he had several weak excuses why he couldn't. Tamara simply said she didn't want to, and left it that.

"So you and *I* will go," said Bennie to Kim.

"And Tamara and I will get ready for Operation Sunlamp on Sunday night," said Theo.

"What?" asked Kim.

"We should have an operation name," said Theo.

"What do you have to get ready?" asked Bennie.

"I have to mentally prepare," said Theo with dignity.

"And you'll have to help me get the lamps on Sunday," said Tamara. "We'll bring them to D and D."

"Oh, okay," said Theo unenthusiastically. "What if your mum catches us?"

"I'll say it was your idea," said Tamara.

"No, wait, that's not—"

"You won't get caught," interrupted Bennie. "Operation Sunlamp is go!"

CHAPTER TWENTY-TWO

Even Bennie had to walk with her bike up the last part of the mountain road, the lowest gear proving not low enough. As Kim had to walk his bike almost from the bottom, he had no sympathy.

"It'll be good going downhill," said Bennie.

"It'll be dangerous," said Kim. He looked up at the sky, where dark clouds hung heavy. They were slowly drifting lower and promised a lot of rain. "Even worse when the road gets wet. Let's look at the mast first, then go to Mrs. Benison's."

"Do we have to actually visit her?" asked Bennie. "I mean, we could just say we did."

"Eila might see her tomorrow or something," said Kim. "Besides, I do want to borrow some books. She's got a whole library."

"Okay, I guess," said Bennie.

They managed to get on their bikes to ride the last fifty yards or so, where the road wasn't so steep. The television mast towered above them, the red light on top blinking again because it had gotten so dark from the clouds.

There was a fence around the mast, topped with concertina barbed wire. Bennie and Kim dropped their bikes and went to look at the gate. Ignoring the warning signs, Bennie tried to open it. Both of them were surprised when the gate easily swung open.

"I guess Aster unlocked it," said Kim. He went to the base of the ladder and looked straight up, a hundred feet or more. The tower was a simple construction of metal struts, so he could see all the way up to the enclosed part at the top, which had several big dishes and a couple of long, pointed aerials mounted on it. "I can't see anything."

"I'm going to take a look," said Bennie. She jumped to grab the lowest rung of the ladder, which was about six feet above the ground, and pulled herself up. "What? No one will be able to see us—the cloud's too low already."

"I don't know," said Kim. He'd always thought he was okay with heights. Now he wasn't so sure.

"Come on." Bennie slapped the rung above her head, which rang like a bell. "Nice, solid ladder."

"All right," replied Kim. Bennie climbed up a ways to give him room. He stepped back to the gate and with a running jump managed to grab hold of the lowest rung and pull himself up effectively, if not with the grace of his friend.

They climbed in silence. Halfway up, they met the cloud coming down, cold wisps of water vapor that made the rungs of the ladder wet and slippery, even before the rain came. Kim gripped even harder and climbed more slowly, being very careful how he placed his feet. Bennie slowed down a little, but not as much, and was soon a dozen rungs ahead.

"There's a trapdoor," she announced.

Kim didn't look up; he didn't want to move his head back and change his center of gravity.

"It's unlocked," said Bennie.

Kim heard a sudden crash of metal on metal. He flinched, pressing himself against the ladder, his knuckles white.

"Wow! There's a kind of—"

Bennie's echoing voice suddenly cut off.

Kim snapped his head back to look up, forgetting about his center-of-gravity concerns. He couldn't see Bennie at all, and for a moment he thought she'd somehow fallen. But he knew that wasn't possible. She had to be up above.

He climbed fast, got to the open trapdoor—the metallic crash must have been it opening—and hauled himself up and through. The platform was enclosed, a steel-walled cabin about fifteen feet a side, full of lockers with electrical and other warning signs stenciled all over them, and another ladder on the far side leading up to a closed trapdoor.

It should have been dark, but it wasn't.

The cabin was full of a soft golden light that came from a strange installation right in the middle, a kind of nest that seemed to be woven out of thick threads of light. It was about two feet high and shaped like an egg with the top cut off; there was as an indentation there exactly the right size for something basketball shaped to fit in. Tendrils of golden light extended from the base of the nest to every locker in the cabin, and up alongside the ladder to the dishes and aerials above.

The golden glow was exactly the same as the light that came from the globe.

Aster's light.

Bennie was crouched down, frozen in place. Her right hand was extended, touching the nest.

"Bennie!" shouted Kim. "Bennie!"

He reached out to pull her arm away, and immediately the cold tendrils of Aster's thought struck, digging into his brain.

Let me in. I am a friend. Let me in.

Kim tried to snatch his hand back. But his fingers were stuck on Bennie's arm. They wouldn't obey him. They wouldn't loosen up and let go.

No, he thought fiercely. *No! You can't come in! You can't! I refuse!*

The nest grew brighter, the light from it fierce on Bennie's face, gold reflecting in her unseeing eyes. Then it dimmed suddenly, and flickered out, the light almost gone for a few moments.

Kim. I'm ... I'm sorry! You have to get away. I don't know how long I can hold Aster ...

That was a new voice inside his mind.

He knew it instantly, even unheard. It was *Eila's* mental voice.

The surprise almost shattered Kim's mental defenses. The golden light suddenly flared back, became blinding, overwhelming his senses. Eila's mental touch faded, and Aster's returned like an unstoppable tide.

Let me in. Let me in. Let me in.

"No!" screamed Kim with voice and mind. His fingers suddenly unlocked and he fell back on the hard steel floor, jarring his elbow.

Bennie didn't move.

"Bennie!" shouted Kim, nursing his elbow. "Aster's not your friend! Fight her! Fight her!"

Kim couldn't tell if his words had any effect. He knew the only thing that would work was to get her hand off the nest. But Aster would reach into his mind again if he touched Bennie, and he was deathly afraid he would not get away a third time.

He looked around helplessly, hoping to see something that would help him. A piece of wood he could push Bennie with. Anything. But there was nothing, and he knew that with every passing second Aster's hold on Bennie would only get stronger.

Ignoring his jarred elbow, Kim settled himself in place next to Bennie, at a right angle. Then he flung himself forward to tackle her around the waist, and threw both of them to the floor.

Bennie screamed, a terrible sound. Kim had never heard her cry out in pain like that. He'd landed half on top of her, and she'd taken the brunt of the collision with the floor.

But she was no longer touching the nest.

"Ah! Ah! Ah!" sobbed his friend. She writhed around, trying to get upright, clutching her left arm by the wrist. Kim slid back from her. His elbow throbbed even more, but otherwise he was okay.

"My shoulder...dislocated..." said Bennie through gritted teeth. Kim vaguely remembered she'd dislocated her shoulder once before, sliding onto a base during a softball game. But he'd only heard about it after; he hadn't been there. "You got to . . . help me get it . . . You pull it forward, straight . . . Grab my wrist."

Kim obeyed, wincing as Bennie flinched with even the slightest movement of her arm.

"Okay, pull steady . . . and straight."

She was pulling on her wrist too, with her right hand, showing him the direction. Kim gave her arm a very tentative pull. He felt sick doing it, seeing the pain on her face.

"A steady, proper pull," said Bennie. She tried to do it herself. Kim got the idea and pulled, as if he was drawing a rowing boat in to the shore by its painter.

There was an audible click. Bennie made a gagging sound and let go, her head lolling forward, but almost instantly looked back up.

"Oh man," she said. She lifted her left arm very slowly, and waggled her fingers. "Thanks for that. And for getting me away from Aster. Again."

"It must be connected to the globe," said Kim, pointing at the nest. It was less bright now, flickering and dimming as if it kept losing power. "And I heard Eila! She said she's trying to hold Aster, whatever that means."

"Yeah," said Bennie. She shook her head. "I kind of heard them struggling. It's hard to describe. It was like Aster was trying to get out of this huge room and Eila kept shutting the doors, only there were so many doors ... At least she's on our side now."

"Maybe," said Kim. "I wish I knew what was happening."

The rain intensified on the roof, heavy drops hammering a constant drumbeat.

"Oh," said Kim, realizing. He had to almost shout to be heard now. "The rain ... It'll be dark enough for Aster to come out. To come here. That's what Eila meant. *You have to get away.*"

CHAPTER TWENTY-THREE

"So let's get away," said Bennie.

"Can you climb with that arm?" asked Kim anxiously.

"Nope," replied Bennie. "But I can climb with the other one."

She laughed as if she'd made a really funny joke.

Then she added, "Only I need you to make a sling with your T-shirt."

"Okay," answered Kim, after a microsecond hesitation. He pulled his T-shirt off, not meeting Bennie's gaze, and wished he'd kept on with the sit-ups. And that he was wearing more clothes. It was much colder now he wasn't climbing, and the sweat and rain felt like it was freezing on his skin.

"Tear it in half," said Bennie. "Twist the pieces into sort of ropes and tie them together into one—"

"I remember how to do it," said Kim, working quickly.

They'd both had first-aid training in Cubs, though they hadn't gone on to Scouts because the local troop had been disbanded—they didn't know why—and the next closest one was too far away for them both, lacking lifts from their parents, due to Kim's not having a car and Bennie's not wanting to help.

"How's that?" asked Kim, tying off the makeshift collar-and-cuff sling behind Bennie's neck.

"It'll do," said Bennie. She paused then said, "You should go first, because you'll be quicker, but I probably need your help to start—"

"Of course!" said Kim. "Slow and steady. You go first."

"At least if I fall, I won't land on you. Help me until I get my feet on the ladder."

Kim held Bennie's right wrist as she swung herself over, balancing on her stomach while she felt for the rungs below.

"It's slippery as anything," muttered Bennie. "Worse than when we came up. Okay, I've got my feet on. Keep holding on, let me down . . . all right . . . I've got a grip on the rung."

"You sure you can do this?" asked Kim anxiously. He slowly released his grip on Bennie's wrist.

"Yep. I've got my arm around the ladder so I can grip using the inside of my elbow and slide that up and down. I'm going to put my head forward over the rung and kind of grip with my chin as well, for when I have to let go—"

"Let go!" exclaimed Kim. "What?"

"Yeah, I can only use one hand, remember." Bennie looked up at him and rolled her eyes. "Step down, chin forward, let go, grab hold next rung, slide elbow down, repeat. It'll be fine."

Kim hadn't thought through how climbing down with one hand would actually work.

"Be careful," he begged. "Don't rush. If you fall, you'll die. Even if Aster does come here, Eila said she doesn't kill."

"I don't think Eila knows what Aster will do," said Bennie. "Let me get about ten rungs down before you follow. See you at the bottom!"

Kim watched through the trapdoor as Bennie looked down, thrust her head forward, and locked her chin over the rung. Then she let go, slid her good arm around the outside of the ladder, and gripped the next rung. She waited a second, then stepped down.

Kim shut his eyes for a second and reminded himself he needed to breathe. He couldn't bear to watch Bennie, knowing he might see her fall, but he couldn't bear to not watch either.

It was almost a relief when he could start down himself, and had to concentrate on his own hand- and footholds. The ladder was much more slippery than it had been. They were sheltered a little bit by the cabin directly overhead, but the rain wasn't coming straight down, and the lower they got, more and more of it came lashing across.

Kim's hands were cold, and his arms and legs far more tired than he'd expected. The climb up had taken more out of him than he thought. But it had to be so much worse for Bennie, climbing with one hand and her chin. Kim had looked down once, but it was difficult and upset his balance, so he didn't try again. Bennie was still on the ladder, about ten rungs below.

He tried not to think about Aster, but couldn't stop himself imagining the globe rolling fast up the hill, maybe even rising up into the air. She could be here in minutes, and then ...

"No, no," he muttered to himself. "Concentrate."

He took a step down and slipped off the rung. He fell, hanging from his handholds and hit his face on the ladder but didn't lose his grip. Scrabbling furiously, he got his feet back on the lower rung and pulled himself close to the ladder, gasping.

"Hey, I'm the one climbing with one hand!" called out Bennie. "You've got no excuse. And you'd knock me off too, so don't fall!"

Kim couldn't answer for at least thirty seconds. He just hung close to the ladder, taking gasping breaths that somehow didn't give him enough air, and he kept swallowing raindrops with them so he had to cough.

"Come on!" Bennie called out again.

It was the quaver in her voice that got him going. She was trying to be her usual self, he knew, brave as anything. But even she couldn't disguise her fear.

"Yeah, yeah!" he croaked, and started down again, pushing his feet wide so that they touched the sides of the ladder as well as getting his soles on the rung. He risked a glimpse over his shoulder, to see how far they'd come, and was shocked to see it was less than halfway.

It was still at least forty feet to the ground. A killing height.

He moved a hand down, tested his grip. His hands were so cold it was hard to tell if his fingers were really tight around the rung or not. He took another step down, shifted his weight. Then another step, moved his left hand down, finding his rhythm again. That's all he had to do, he told himself.

Keep up the rhythm, one handhold, one step, simply keep moving, don't think about falling, or Aster rolling up to zap them both. Only the rhythm of the movement. One, two, one, two, one, two—

He heard a thud and a cry of pain. He craned his neck and looked down. Bennie was on the ground. But she hadn't fallen; she'd just dropped from the bottom of the ladder. Kim only had about ten rungs to go.

"I made it!" shouted Bennie. The rain was lashing across her, and one of the lights on the fence shone behind her, creating a halo effect around her head. She raised her good arm and punched the sky. "Yee-haw!"

Kim kept up his rhythm, hung on the last rung with both hands, and dropped to the ground. Bennie gave him a one-armed hug as he stood there, shivering, his bare torso gleaming with sweat and rain.

"Mrs. Benison's . . ." he sputtered. "Got to get warm . . . clothes."

CHAPTER TWENTY-FOUR

They hurried along the road to Mrs. Benison's house, heads down to keep the rain out of their eyes. But both kept darting glances to either side, each knowing they were looking out for the golden glow of the globe. The rain was so heavy even a light might not be seen until it was very close. Too close . . .

Mrs. Benison's house was hard to see in the rain. There didn't seem to be any lights on. Kim knocked on the door, while Bennie shook herself like a dog, spraying droplets all over the veranda before suddenly groaning and clutching her shoulder.

"Forgot about that," she said.

There was no answer to Kim's knock.

"Is she deaf?" asked Bennie. "Knock harder."

"I don't think so. She's always heard me before," said Kim. He rapped the knocker again, much more loudly. "Maybe the rain is too heavy."

He tried the door handle. It turned, and he pushed the door partly open.

"Hi, Mrs. Benison!" he called out. "It's Kim Basalt! Can I come in? I have a friend with me."

There was no answer, and there was no light on in the hall.

"Can you hear that?" asked Bennie.

"What?"

"I dunno, a kind of humming sound," said Bennie. "Very low."

"All I can hear is the rain on the roof," said Kim. He shouted now, as loud as he could, "Mrs. Benison! It's me, Kim!"

There was still no answer.

"Come on, we have to get dry and warm," said Bennie. She slid past Kim and went on down the hall. Kim hurried to catch up with her.

"Kitchen straight ahead," he said. "She'll probably be there or the library. That's the door on the left."

Bennie carried on to the kitchen, and cautiously opened the door. But she didn't go in. Over her shoulder, Kim saw Mrs. Benison slumped in a chair by the kitchen table. There was a portable radio in front of the old lady, and she had one hand on it.

"Is she dead?" whispered Kim.

"I don't know!" Bennie whispered back. "No, look—she's breathing. She's asleep."

Gingerly, they stepped into the kitchen.

"That sound is coming from the radio," said Bennie.

"I can't hear it," said Kim.

Bennie stepped a little closer, but retreated immediately, and put her fingers in her ears, wincing as she lifted her left arm to do so.

"It's not a sound," she said, too loudly. "It's inside my head. But it is coming from that radio. It's . . . it's Aster. She wants me to, to—"

Kim pulled her back into the hall.

Bennie took her fingers out of her ears.

"Turn it off," she said. "I can still . . . It's still getting to me."

Kim ran back into the kitchen and grabbed the radio. It was off. As he looked at the dials, he suddenly heard or sensed the hum. It was like a low, threatening growl that slowly resolved into Aster's mental voice.

This is an emergency broadcast. You must listen carefully. Make sure you are in a safe place to listen. Prepare for further instructions. This is an emergency broadcast. You must listen carefully. Make sure you are in a safe place to listen. Prepare for further instructions.

"Kim!"

Bennie's shout brought Kim back to his senses. He found himself already sitting down next to Mrs. Benison, with the radio in his hand. He turned the power button again, on and then off, but it didn't do anything. The voice was still there. He could feel himself slipping into a daze. It was very peaceful to sit and wait for someone to tell him what to do . . .

Something hit him on the shoulder. Kim recovered from the daze. The radio was back on the table. He grabbed it, found the battery compartment, fumbled the cover off, and smacked the radio against the table. The batteries flew out, and Aster's mental voice was cut off.

Kim rubbed his shoulder. There was a red imprint there, all wavy lines. The tread from a sneaker. He looked down. Bennie had thrown her shoe at him.

"Nice tattoo," she said, coming in. She retrieved her waterlogged shoe and shook it, spraying Kim with water. "If Aster can do her mind control over the radio, there'll be a lot of people asleep like Mrs. Benison . . ."

"I bet she can do it through televisions too," said Kim. "That's why she wanted one at our place." He looked at the radio. "And it doesn't matter if they're turned off."

"Theo must be right after all," said Bennie. She opened the tin that was on the table and shoveled two Nice biscuits into her mouth, spraying crumbs as she continued. "Aster *is* leading an alien invasion."

"We have to get back to my place," said Kim. "Find out what's going on. Help Eila."

"Eat something first," said Bennie, cramming another biscuit in her mouth. "And we need dry clothes, at least on top. You particularly."

"We should try the phone in the hall," said Kim. He looked at the old lady. She seemed only asleep, but every now and then her inward breath stuttered. "Call an ambulance for Mrs. Benison."

"I bet it doesn't work," said Bennie. She was looking in the fridge now. "Everyone will be knocked out. Or Aster will have done something else."

Bennie was right. The phone didn't work.

Kim went back to the kitchen to eat a biscuit, even though he found he was almost too stressed out to eat anything, then they went in search of clothes.

Ten minutes later, they were back outside. Kim had replaced his missing T-shirt with a red silk blouse, not caring. Both had huge tweed coats on, the only things left in what they presumed was Mr. Benison's wardrobe. The coats were very heavy, but also very warm and water-resistant. They'd found golf umbrellas and taken one each. Bennie's umbrella had TOOTHS BEER printed all over it in giant red letters, and Kim's had a big black swan without a brand name at all.

"We'd better take the road," said Kim. "The bush track'll be too muddy and slippery."

He'd already dismissed Bennie's suggestion that he ride ahead by himself, as she didn't think she could ride one-handed down the mountain.

"What'll we even do when we do get back?" asked Bennie.

"I don't know." Kim was desperately worried for everyone, but most particularly for Eila.

"I wish I had sword," said Bennie. "A magic sword that could cut Aster."

"Magic swords don't exist," said Kim.

"Well, we didn't think beings like Aster did either, before," said Bennie.

Kim didn't answer. He just walked a bit faster.

"Maybe we should run for a while," said Bennie.

"It won't hurt your shoulder?" asked Kim. He really wanted to run himself. He wanted to get home and find out what was going on. He felt like there might be something he could do, if only he could get home fast enough.

"Not too much," said Bennie. She started to jog, and tangled her umbrella with Bennie's for a moment before moving farther away. "Let's lose the umbrellas!"

She threw her umbrella high, off the side of the

mountain. The wind caught it and it sailed up and away, twirling through the bands of rain before starting to fall.

Kim threw his too, but it didn't get caught up by the wind. It simply plunged down the mountainside until it was caught in the branches of a tree. He broke into a jog, catching up to Bennie so they ran side by side in the middle of the road.

CHAPTER TWENTY-FIVE

"There's someone moving around," said Bennie.

They were crouched down behind a very thick-trunked gum tree close to the perimeter fence of the experimental farm. The gate, Kim noted, was open.

"Where?" he asked.

"Front of the shed. See?"

Kim peered through the sheets of rain.

"Is that Tamara?" he asked, surprised.

"Yeah, it is," confirmed Bennie.

Tamara was scanning the hillside, slowly turning her head.

"You reckon Aster's taken control of her?" asked Bennie.

"How would I know?"

Someone joined Tamara. Kim and Bennie squinted.

"That's Theo," said Bennie. "What do you think? Should we go in?"

"I dunno..." Kim started to say, but Bennie had stood up at the same time a third, smaller person joined Theo and Tamara at the front of the shed, all of them standing just inside enough to avoid the rain.

"That's Madir," said Bennie. "Come on!"

She hurried forward. A few seconds later, Kim followed. They'd only gone a few yards when there was a happy cry from the shed and Madir came running out like a bullet, followed by Tamara. Theo stayed in the shed, out of the rain.

"Bennie!" squealed Madir. "Oh, you're hurt!"

"It's nothing, squirt." Bennie gave her sister a one-armed hug. "I dislocated my arm again, but Kim helped me put it back. What's going on?"

"A lot," said Tamara. "Eila says we only have about two hours. We have to move quickly. Come on!"

"Two hours for what?" asked Kim. "Is she okay?"

"Sort of," said Tamara. "Uh, this rain!"

"About time you got here," said Theo as they reached the shed. The rain was very noisy on the tin roof.

"Where's Eila?" asked Kim. "What's happening?"

"She'll explain," said Tamara, hurrying ahead. "Come on!"

They raced through the kitchen, toward Eila's room. Kim paused by the living room door. He could see his parents sitting on the lounge, apparently asleep. The new television was silent, its power cord pulled out of the wall socket, obviously too late.

"Is everyone asleep?" asked Kim somberly.

"I think so," said Tamara. "We were too, but Eila called to us, broke us out. Told us to come here. Come on, she can't often talk for long."

Kim tore his gaze away from his parents. He was so used to them taking control of everything, being sure they knew what was the right thing to do. Now they were unconscious, under the control of an alien globe.

Eila was sitting cross-legged on her bed, holding the globe on her lap, her fingers interlaced for a better grip. The golden glow was patchy, bright in some places, dark in others. There were also lines of that same light spreading up Eila's fingers into her hands, but even as Kim watched, some of them ebbed back and faded, while others intensified and advanced a tiny distance.

Kim. Bennie. Good.

Eila's voice sounded inside Kim's head. Her mouth didn't move at all; there was no sound.

I'm sorry, Kim. I misunderstood Aster. Everything's gone wrong.

"What . . . what can we do?" asked Kim.

I am in a mental battle with Aster. We are almost equally strong, and I can utilize many of her powers. But I will weaken before she does because my body will fail. You have to get the globe where the sun can see it. Before nightfall.

"Where the sun can see it? We can get sunlamps from

Tamara's mum's pharmacy. That won't take—"

No. A sunlamp will do nothing. It is not the light itself. I don't know why, but Aster does not want to be 'seen' by the sun.

"It's raining cats and dogs out there!" protested Bennie. "There can't be any sun for miles!"

Aster has made the rain heavier, but I have brought a wind from the north. This band of rain is no more than five miles wide. It will be pushed to the south. We must go east or west, as quickly as possible, to catch the sun. You will have to carry me. I cannot physically let go of Aster or she will mentally break free as well.

"Okay, who can drive a car?" asked Theo. "Besides me? I sort of can. I think."

A car won't work. I cannot stop all of Aster's powers all the time. She can control electricity locally, including car batteries.

"How far do we need to go?" asked Kim.

Until you reach sunshine. I must stop talking. Aster is trying something—

"Two hours three minutes till sunset," said Theo, looking at his watch.

A loud thump in the hall made them all jump. It was followed by heavy footsteps, and a second later Darwin appeared in the doorway. He was unsteady on his feet and gripped the doorway with his left hand. In his right hand he held the broomstick that Kim and Bennie had broken, brandishing it like a sword.

Darwin swung his head from side to side, as if seeing something entirely different from the children in front of him. His wide-open eyes were entirely gold, the same color as the globe, but it was a dead, solid gold without internal light.

"Plant thieves," muttered Darwin. "Plant thieves!"

He stepped into the room and raised the broomstick, ready to bring it down directly on Eila's head. But before he could, Kim launched himself forward, grabbed his arm and swung it, yelling, "Dad! Don't! It's Eila!"

Theo threw himself on Darwin's left leg, while Tamara grabbed his right. Still he moved forward, dragging them with him. He tried to shake Kim off, swinging his arm back, but Kim held tight and pulled his legs up so he was a deadweight.

Bennie grabbed Darwin's left thumb with her good hand and pulled it back. But none of it stopped him. He shook Bennie off, transferred the broomstick to his left hand and struck at Eila while the tangled, confusing melee continued.

But the blow landed on Madir, who'd jumped in the way. The stick hit her shielding arms with a hideous crack and she crumpled to the ground. Bennie cried out and kicked at Darwin's shins, Kim tried to drag him down, Theo and Tamara tried to bend his knees.

But he was too big and too strong. The stick went up again.

But it did not come down.

Darwin froze in place.

I have broken Aster's control of Dad. We must move, quickly! Avoid people. She can call on anyone nearby who has heard or seen her order to wait for instructions.

Bennie was checking Madir's arms. The younger girl was shivering, clearly in shock.

"Not broken, I think," said Bennie. "Badly bruised. Lucky it was his left hand."

Kim slowly let go of his father's arm. He looked up into Darwin's frozen face. His eyes were normal now, but open and unseeing. It was horrible.

"Is Mum going to attack us too?" he asked.

No. Aster tried, but she is more resistant. I cannot talk. Go!

"East or west, and at least five miles," said Theo, picking himself up. "We can't use a car. In under two hours now. Carrying Eila and the globe. Bennie's hurt; so is Madir."

"We know," said Tamara. "Don't be negative."

"I'm just establishing the parameters," protested Theo.

"East or west," said Kim. "And we have to go quickly, and avoid people. No motors. The wind will be from the north."

"Yeah, so I missed a couple of parameters—" Theo began.

"The lake!" continued Kim. "We go down to the university yacht club, take one of their Corsairs, that'll fit us all. Sail east up the lake to the river, and along the river as far as we need to go."

"Brilliant!" exclaimed Bennie. "Only how do we get Eila and the globe down to the yacht club?"

CHAPTER TWENTY-SIX

"This is really hard work," panted Theo. He was pushing the big farm wheelbarrow, the one with the proper inflated car tire. Eila was in the wheelbarrow, sitting on a cushion, Aster still held firmly in her lap.

"Five more minutes, then it's Kim's turn again," said Bennie, looking at her glowing watch.

"We'll be there in five minutes!" gasped Theo.

Bennie didn't answer. They were making their way down one of the backstreets of the university campus, in theory avoiding the places where lots of people might be waiting, ready to be taken over by Aster. That meant staying off the main road, which had lots of student residences, and away from the restaurant and shops area.

The rain was easing, as Eila had promised, but they were all soaking wet already. Kim and Bennie had ditched the sodden tweed coats for some of Kim's tracksuit tops, which were much lighter but nowhere near as warm. The wind from the north was cold and gusty, but it gave them a bit of a boost while they were headed south to the yacht club.

They hadn't seen anyone awake. Aster's radio and

television instructions appeared to have made everybody go inside and settle down, though they had seen one man sitting on a park bench with a radio by his side. They steered well away from him, and he didn't move.

"Okay, not far," said Kim. They were passing the vice-chancellor's house, an impressive white-painted 1920s edifice, and could see the lake behind the garden. "I'll take over."

Theo set the wheelbarrow down and stepped back, inspecting his palms.

"Oh, I've got bad blisters," he said. He was about to say something else but stopped as Bennie made a sad face and pointed at her own shoulder and Madir's badly bruised arms.

Kim lifted the wheelbarrow and pushed.

She's doing something, Eila reported. *I can't tell... calling someone to come here...*

"The alien fleet?" asked Theo. "She's a scout, right?"

No. There is no fleet. Someone about a mile away. Two of them. Police officers. She has control. They're coming. They will shoot us.

"I thought you said Aster doesn't kill!" shouted Kim, pushing harder.

I didn't understand. Aster thinks this is all a game.

"What!"

I must concentrate. I will try to break her hold on the police. She's trying something else too. Hurry!

Kim tried to push the wheelbarrow even faster. But it was harder than it should be. For a moment he thought the tire must have blown. Then he saw Eila struggling to hold the globe, which had fallen between her legs and was resting on the bottom of the wheelbarrow. She still had her hands on it, and was gripping it with her knees.

"The globe's gone heavy," he cried. "Eila, you have to make Aster light again!"

There was no answer.

"Help me, guys!" panted Kim. If the wheelbarrow stopped completely he didn't think they'd be able to get it going again. They had to maintain momentum.

Theo and Tamara went to either side and pushed. Bennie dangerously went to the front and pulled with her good hand. The wheelbarrow kept moving.

In the distance, they heard the wail of a police siren, rising and falling.

I cannot break her hold on the police. I will try to make the globe less dense.

"Bennie, get out of the way!" shouted Kim, just in time. Bennie skipped aside as the wheelbarrow suddenly got lighter again and picked up speed.

"Tamara, run ahead and check that Corsair tied up on the jetty," panted Kim. "Or whatever that is behind it—anything big enough for the six of us."

He knew Tamara was a sailor. They'd learned together one summer, all of them, though only Tamara had kept it up, because her parents owned a yacht. It was big enough too, but moored on the other side of the lake, at the ritzier yacht club.

"I'll help," said Theo. He and Tamara sprinted ahead, across the parking lot and past the white-painted tin shed that was the rudimentary clubhouse. There were a lot of small sailing dinghies pulled up on the beach next to the clubhouse, but they were all too small. There were half a dozen larger boats out in the small bay, but there was no time to row out to them. They needed one of the two boats tied up to the jetty.

The police siren was getting closer. Kim grunted as he pushed the wheelbarrow off the road, across the top of the concrete boat ramp, and then with even more effort, up an inch or so onto the wooden jetty.

Tamara was raising the foresail on the Corsair. Theo held the boat against the jetty. Kim pushed the wheelbarrow up next to it and looked down at them.

"Theo, swap with Madir," said Kim. "Mad, are your

arms okay? Can you hold the boat against the jetty?"

"Yep," Madir replied bravely, climbing down into the yacht.

"I'll help," said Bennie. She looked back. "Sorry I can't lift Eila."

"No worries," snapped out Kim. "Theo. We're going to have to lift her up under the arms and put her on the side of the jetty. Then I'll go aboard and you kind of slide her down to me. Okay?"

"Um, yeah," said Theo nervously. He looked back along the jetty. The police siren was sounding awfully close now.

It was hard to lift Eila out, and Kim wished he'd thought to point the wheelbarrow at the boat and tip her slowly to the jetty, but he didn't think of it until he and Theo were already lifting her up.

"Eila, hold the globe tight!" said Kim. "Guys, make sure the boat stays close."

They got Eila onto the jetty. Kim immediately dropped down into the boat and turned back, lifting his arms. Theo got behind Eila and lifted her again under the arms, pushing her forward. Kim reached for her, keeping his knees bent. He felt really unsteady, and his legs ached from climbing the tower and pushing the barrow.

"You got her?" asked Theo.

"Ye . . . yes," panted Kim. He did a kind of controlled

collapse, sitting down in the bottom of the boat, with Eila on top. She still had the globe clasped to her stomach.

"Cast off!" shouted Tamara. "Get in, Theo!"

Theo climbed in. Madir and Bennie pushed hard against the jetty. The boat veered away, and Tamara, sitting back at the tiller, reached out to ease the foresail sheet, letting it billow out and catch the wind. The boat began to move purposefully through the water.

"Get the main up!" ordered Tamara. She looked back over her shoulder. They could all hear how close the police siren was, and now they saw the car shooting past the vice-chancellor's house, blue lights flashing.

Kim, and Bennie one-handed, hauled on the main halyard with grim ferocity. The sail shot up, filling as it rose. The wind was on their quarter as Tamara steered southeast, to pick up speed as quickly as possible.

"Theo, main sheet!" roared Tamara.

Theo was already on the rope, hauling hard, with Madir tailing off the sheet.

The wind gusted, and the boat heeled over, sending Bennie into Kim, and Madir into Theo. Tamara eased the tiller, decreasing the pressure. Throughout, Eila sat like a rock in the middle, the globe clutched between her knees.

Behind them, the police car screeched to a

rubber-burning halt next to the clubhouse. The doors flew open and two police officers jumped out, already drawing their pistols.

"Down! Everyone get down!" shouted Bennie, crouching low.

CHAPTER TWENTY-SEVEN

Shots echoed over the lake. *Crack-crack-crack-crack!*

The echoes faded. There was only the sound of the wind, the creaking of the boat, the slap of the water on the bow, the groan of the rigging. The yacht was flying now, speeding away.

"Anyone . . anyone hit?" asked Kim. His question came out as a squeak, he was so afraid of the answer. He lifted himself up a little and looked back over the gunwale. They were already farther away than he'd thought. The two police officers were standing at the end of the jetty, pistols down by their sides. As he watched, they turned and ran back toward their car.

"We're okay," said Bennie. She was checking over Eila, who had not moved. "Mad?"

"I'm all right," whispered Madir.

"Me too," said Theo. "Amazingly."

"Check the hull to port," said Tamara. "I turned us to put it higher—they might have hit there."

"Can't see any holes," said Kim. "How did they miss?"

They did not want to shoot. Aster tried to compel both of them and lost total control. We must hurry. She is bringing another band of rain, piggybacking on the wind I raised.

"Oh man, couldn't she be a bit stupider?" complained Bennie.

There was no response from Eila.

"They're following us on land," said Tamara. "If they get to the first bridge before we do, they can shoot us from above. Easily."

"Can we sail any faster?" Kim asked.

"I don't think so. We can trim the boat a bit, but these Corsairs are heavy. You sit to port, Kim, and Theo. Uh, and Madir too."

I can increase the wind a little. But that will help Aster bring the rain faster.

"I reckon we have to," said Kim. He could see the flashing blue light of the police car between university buildings. At least it would be slowed down a bit in the campus maze, but all too soon they'd be out of there. "Tamara?"

"Uh, not too much, Eila," said Tamara nervously.

I don't know sailing. How about ten percent stronger?

"Uh, yes, I guess, but don't make it—"

The wind suddenly gusted hard, making the boat heel over, the starboard gunwales almost in the water. For a second it looked like they'd capsize, as Bennie threw herself to port to add her weight and the others all leaned out as far as they could.

"Gust!" shouted Tamara, easing off the main sheet. "Don't make it gust!"

Sorry. Steady now.

The boat leaned back to port. Tamara made more adjustments to tiller and sheets, until they were scudding along even faster than before.

"If we were racing, this'd be one of the best six-person-crew times ever," said Tamara.

"Just so long as we get past the bridge before those two cops," said Bennie. "Can you see them, Kim?"

"Nope. Maybe some of the roads are blocked. There must have been a lot of drivers who just stopped when they heard Aster's message."

"Good point," said Theo. "Let's hope so."

"The sky is clearer to the east," said Kim. "I can almost see blue."

"I wonder what'll happen when Aster gets 'seen by the sun,'" said Theo, looking past the bow. "Yeah, it is clear sky ahead!"

"Maybe she'll fall into ashes, like a vampire," said Bennie enthusiastically.

"Eila?" asked Kim.

Do not distract me. I don't know. I only know Aster does not want the attention of the sun.

"Bridge ahead," said Tamara. "Anyone see the police car?"

There was a chorus of "No."

"I'll steer north of the center span," said Tamara. "Closer for them, but faster sailing. Okay?"

"You're the captain," said Kim.

"Right," said Tamara. "Hold the tiller for a sec, Kim. Same point."

Kim edged back and took the tiller, keeping the course. Tamara whipped a cloth out of her pocket and cleaned her glasses. Almost as soon as she put them back on they had collected a dozen raindrops on each lens, although the rain was now not much more than a drizzle.

"I see the cop car!" Bennie called out. "We'll get past ahead of them."

"We need to get well past," said Theo. "We'll be sitting ducks if they're shooting down at us from the bridge."

"I think they can't get past something," said Bennie. "There's two buses stopped next to each other ... yeah ... I can't see the car but the light is going backward. They're crossing over to come up the wrong side of the road."

They were almost under the bridge now. For a second it looked like the mast was too high, and would hit, but Kim knew this was an optical illusion. Twenty seconds later, they sailed out the other side and were rushing headlong east, toward the open sky and the sun.

"The second bridge is closer for us," said Tamara. "Is it closer for them?"

"I can't see them," said Bennie. "But they'll have to cross back over and go through Civic. That should be slow—there'd be a lot of stopped cars. And buses."

"How far ahead is that clear sky, do you reckon?" asked Kim. "Before the end of the lake, where the river comes in?"

The others all peered ahead.

"Nuh, I don't think so," said Bennie.

"I was hoping we could just sail into the sunshine," said Kim. "We won't be able to get very far up the river. Once we're out of the boat, we'll be slow. I don't even know how we'll carry Eila and the globe."

"Two of us make a seat with our arms," said Bennie. "Sorry. Two of you. I wish I hadn't done my shoulder in."

"We have to get there first," said Theo.

"Is that someone under Aster's control?" asked Tamara urgently. A man on the far shore was waving his fishing rod at them and calling out something.

"Don't think so," said Kim. "There's bound to be a few

people who didn't hear the radio or see a TV, or get called in by other people to listen. Must be pretty weird for them."

"Don't worry!" shouted Bennie, over the water. "We're saving the world! Keep fishing!"

"I doubt he heard you over the wind," said Kim.

Whether he heard or not, the man kept shouting and waving his fishing rod as they sped past. They couldn't hear what he was shouting.

There was a definite end to the cloud cover ahead, and the rain had almost stopped. But looking north, there was another band of dark, rain-heavy cloud, moving fast. Also to the north, a mile or two away, they could see a flashing blue light, even if the wind carried away the sound of the siren.

CHAPTER TWENTY-EIGHT

"We're aground," said Tamara, as the boat shuddered to a slow, grating halt, well short of the riverbank she'd been aiming for. She'd already lowered the main, and now that she let the foresail sheet go, the sail flapped uselessly in the breeze.

They were so close. The sky was completely clear only a few hundred yards to the east, and the sun was shining down. There was even a faint rainbow, though it seemed more like a mockery than a sign of good luck to them.

The riverbanks were crowded with bulrushes, which had slowed the boat. They were at least fifteen feet from the shore, and though the boat was aground, the water was still at least five feet deep.

"We'll have to swim," said Kim. "Too slow to try to get through the bulrushes."

He pointed ahead up the river, to the ramp used by the waterskiing powerboats. They skimmed the surface and could go much farther up the river than any yacht. "We can't get out before the boat ramp."

"But Eila and the globe!" protested Madir.

"We'll put a life jacket on Eila and tow her," said Kim. "Bennie, you put one on too. They're under the forepeak, right?"

Bennie went forward and opened the cover, pulling out two bulky yellow life jackets and throwing them back.

"Anyone else want one?" asked Kim. "Everyone can swim?"

Swimming lessons were compulsory at school, so he would have been amazed if anyone had said they couldn't.

"I don't really need a life jacket," protested Bennie. "I reckon I can just do a kind of sidestroke—"

"Put on one, just in case," said Kim. He started to put the life jacket on Eila. Her eyes were shut and she didn't react at all to the jacket going over her head.

"Eila, you're going to have to lift one hand off the globe and put it through the armhole, then the other," he said. "Can you see or . . . uh . . . sense what we're doing?"

I can see through your eyes. All of you. There is a risk if I release my hand, it will lessen my control over Aster. But I see I have to. Be ready.

"No, no, wait! Everyone else, go over the side now," said Kim.

"Shoes and jackets off first," said Tamara.

Kim nodded, shrugged himself out of his tracksuit top, and started taking his shoes off.

"What if you need help?" Bennie asked. She tucked her sneakers into the waist of her tracksuit pants, one by one, flinching as she bent down. Everyone else just dropped their shoes where they were.

"You can climb back on," said Kim. "If she zaps everybody all at once, we're finished."

"Good point," said Bennie. She clipped her life jacket closed and went over the side, a few seconds behind everyone else. Kim ignored the splashes, and bent over his sister and the globe.

"Okay, Eila. Left side first. On three. One . . . two . . . three!"

Eila jerked her hand away from the globe and thrust it to the side. Kim guided her fingers through the armhole, and Eila shoved her hand through and around, back on the globe a second later.

"So far so good," said Kim. "Ready for your right hand? On three. One . . . two . . . three!"

Eila's hand shot out. At the same time, the globe flew forward, striking Kim in the stomach. Eila clawed it back with her left hand, but even as she did so, Kim was hit with a bolt of blue electricity that threw him back over the stern and into the water.

He blacked out for a second, but the second shock from

the chill of the water brought him back. He came spluttering up, his arms smashing big strokes to get his head out. His chest hurt like crazy and he couldn't breathe. He started to panic, sucking in water as much as air, his arms windmilling the river until they were gripped on either side, and he panicked even more until he processed that it was Theo and Tamara, trying to hold him up.

"Lie back!" shouted Tamara. "Relax!"

Kim tried to obey, coughing and spewing water out of his mouth, fighting the urge to keep thrashing with his arms.

"Keep still, idiot!"

That was Bennie, holding up his head with her good hand and kicking hard below.

Kim finally got a breath in without water coming with it. He coughed and quietened down, letting himself float.

"Eila?" he gasped.

"Mad's doing up her life jacket," said Bennie. "She's got a good hold on the globe again. You okay?"

"Yeah," gasped Kim. "We have to hurry, get Eila in the water—"

"We're on it," said Tamara. "Can you tread water now? Better stay back from the boat."

"Yeah," gasped Kim again. He leaned forward, let his

legs drop, and started the cycling motion that would keep him afloat.

Kim felt Tamara and Theo let him go. He blinked furiously to clear his eyes, and saw them climb back aboard. He kicked harder and did a few backstrokes to get a bit farther away from the boat so he'd have a clearer view of what was going on.

This also gave him a view of the stormfront coming in from the north. It could only be minutes away, and looking around, he saw ripples on the water from the rising wind. Aster had clearly taken over the weather from Eila.

But there was still blue sky only a hundred yards or so away, and sunshine with it.

There was a loud splash, followed by two more. Kim looked back to the boat. Eila was bobbing in the water, the globe held high up her chest. The life jacket, designed for an adult, was working, but the water was almost up to Eila's chin.

"Tow her!" croaked Kim. He turned onto his front and started to breaststroke. He was much faster using freestyle, but he wanted to see what was going on. "Hurry!"

Theo and Tamara gripped a loop on each side of the life jacket and began to swim, both of them backstroking, using one arm. Kim swam up close to them, followed by

Bennie, who was slower in the life jacket and with only one arm. Madir kept close to her sister's side.

The water was cold, but Kim was beyond caring about that now. He felt like he might never get warm again, but it didn't matter. They just had to get Eila to the boat ramp and up it, and carry her and the globe through the dirt car park beyond and into the little meadow he'd seen from the boat, with the shaft of afternoon sunlight slanting down to light it up.

They had just reached the bottom of the ramp and Theo and Tamara were crawling up the slippery, weedy surface with great care, pulling Eila behind them, when the police car arrived at the top.

An unmarked Z-plated white Ford, with no flashing blue light, no siren, and no warning.

A single officer got out.

Chief Inspector Benison, her eyes dull gold. The champion pistol shooter, who'd shot a crocodile in the eye at about the same distance she was from Eila now.

She already had her pistol out, steady in a two-handed grip. She raised it, looked down over the sights and—

CHAPTER TWENTY-NINE

Bennie threw her shoe. It struck exactly where she aimed, between Inspector Benison's eyes. The police officer fell backward and fired wild, the bullet going off somewhere to the right. She put one hand down and tried to get up again, but lost her footing on the slimy boat ramp and slipped back, smacking her head.

"Get Eila up the ramp!" shouted Kim. He almost slipped on the weedy ramp himself, even though he was already on his hands and knees. He cut his palm on something, but he didn't care, dashing forward as fast he could. He got to Inspector Benison as the woman tried to get up once again, and tore the pistol out of her weak grasp, turning to throw it into the river. She tried to fight him, but Bennie and Madir arrived and knelt on her arms. She subsided back, and the gold ebbed away to show her staring, unseeing eyes.

A heavy raindrop splashed on Kim's forehead. He looked up and saw a curtain of rain sweeping down. The stormfront was almost upon them.

Kim. Take the globe into the sun. I'm going to hit her with everything I can in about a second. She'll be stunned for a while. I hope. There is no more time. I'm sorry for everything.

Kim whirled around. Theo and Tamara, still on all fours, had dragged Eila halfway up the ramp. They were bending over, ready to haul again when two huge sparks flew out of the globe and knocked them both over, onto their backs. They lay there gasping.

Eila stood up, turned around, threw the globe to Kim, and toppled over, sliding down the ramp.

Kim caught the globe instinctively, tucking it into his chest. Aster was completely dark now, and light as a basketball. He spun on one foot and took off, almost falling forward as one foot slipped. But he recovered, and ran on, off the ramp. He ran through the mud of the parking lot, jumping over the low wooden barrier there to stop cars driving farther, and ran on into the meadow.

Rain chased him, and the shaft of sunshine ahead seemed to shrink and move farther away. Kim pumped his tired legs, leaned forward, and gave it everything he had.

Aster struck. Not with electricity. He felt the cold tendrils reaching into his mind. This time she was not trying to communicate. She was feeling for the nerves that controlled his legs, his lungs, his heart. She was trying to stop him, make his legs fail, collapse his lungs, stop his heart.

But she was too late.

With a huge, final leap, Kim reached the sunshine and raised the globe above his head.

Aster's mental intrusion shriveled like a drop of water on a hot frying pan. Kim gasped as he realized she had managed to close his throat at the last second. He sucked in air and kept his arms up, kept the globe in the sun.

It began to shine, growing brighter and brighter, impossibly bright.

Then there was a full second of total darkness, the sun in the sky and the sun in his hands both gone.

Kim blinked. He wasn't holding anything. Aster was gone. He was still standing in sunshine, but it faded as the clouds above rolled across and the rain came down once more.

He dropped his arms, and then dropped to his knees, still gasping, the rain drumming a constant beat upon his back, rivulets of water running around his neck.

Kim felt something touch his mind again, a hideous, unexpected, awful surprise.

???????QuerymeansofCommunicationAcceptable????

No, thought Kim fiercely. *No! Not again! Get out of my head!*

He felt a sudden, incredibly sharp pain behind his eyes for a moment, then the mental voice was gone.

"I see," he heard. "I must apologize."

It was Mrs. Benison's voice.

Kim looked up. The rain had been pushed aside as if an invisible shelter vastly larger than the golf umbrellas they'd borrowed had suddenly been extended above them.

Mrs. Benison was standing in front him. Or rather, a being made of the same golden light as Aster, in the shape of Mrs. Benison, was standing in front of him. Only she was about ten feet tall and her feet were floating a foot above the ground.

"This semblance is calming for you, I think?" asked the shining Mrs. Benison.

"Um, I guess so," muttered Kim. He heard something behind him and snapped his head around to look, making his neck twinge. He ignored it, like all the other pains in his body.

Bennie was there, holding her remaining shoe in her hand, ready to throw. Theo and Tamara were a bit behind her, half carrying Eila, with Madir helping them. They all seemed to be sort of okay.

Alive, at least. For now.

"Who are you?" asked Kim.

"I am the . . . let me see . . . mother . . . of the entity you called Aster. I wish to thank you for preventing my . . .

child . . . committing acts that would require serious adjustment."

"Your child!" exclaimed Kim.

"Yes," said the shining being. "Aster is of a maturity of an equivalence to ten of your years."

"Ten years old," said Kim. He shook his head and swallowed down something halfway between a laugh and a sob. *"Ten years old."*

"Aster was, of course, forbidden to enter your . . . hum . . . eventuality, dimension, continuum," continued the being. "Aster did not understand that you are, in your own small way, sentient beings."

"Aster thought it was a game," said Eila, who had come up next to her brother. She looked at Kim. "Like your D and D. And all of us pieces, including me. When I thought we were learning together, she was just learning how to play with us."

"Our ten-year-old overlord," said Theo. "What was she going to do with everyone she had waiting for instructions?"

The golden being was silent. Eventually, Eila spoke.

"I think," she said wearily, "she was going to make us all fight each other."

"But this did not take place," said the glowing giant woman.

"What happens now, then?" asked Kim.

"I have expressed my... gratitude... and will now depart," said Aster's mother.

"What!" shouted Kim. "Your daughter could have killed us! Maybe she has killed a bunch of people already with her mind control and how are we going to explain... how..."

"Yeah," said Bennie. "You owe us for your kid's rotten behavior."

"I cannot unmake what has been made," said the entity. She paused, and her head turned completely around on her shoulders, her eyes flashing. "And no one has died. No one as a result of Aster's actions. It is possible some will die. The loss of sentient life is not optimal. It is regretted."

"You said you cannot unmake what has been made," said Kim. "But can you... Are you allowed to make something new? I mean, do what Aster did, but to make things better? I'm thinking—"

"Kim," Eila interrupted. "That's where I went wrong."

"Your sister has grown a little wiser," said Not Mrs. Benison. "But I think some minor adjustment is, in fact, called for—"

She paused, and bent her head down, looking straight at Madir.

"What, child? You want me to appear as a huge golden lion? A male one, with a mane. Why?"

"Yes, please," said Madir, as Bennie cried out, "No! No!"

"You're fine as you are," said Kim hastily. "What do you mean, an adjustment?"

"A small one," said the entity. "With my thanks."

She suddenly grew enormous wings, which towered up behind her. The wings swept forward and gathered them all up, and then everyone was gone. The meadow was empty, and the rain came down again.

EPILOGUE

"So you're a paladin, Eila," said Kim. "And Madir, it's fine to be a thief. But are you sure?"

"Yes," said Eila. "I want to fight for what is right. In the game, I mean. I'm over it in real life."

Kim shared a look with Bennie, who raised her eyebrows, and her wrist, which was now in a proper collar-and-cuff sling.

"And I want to steal stuff," said Madir. "For the group, that is."

They were all in Bennie's garage, on the next Sunday afternoon. They'd only just ushered out Mr. and Mrs. Chance, who'd brought in sandwiches and drinks and were still being lovey-dovey with each other and all too interested in what their children were doing. But they had finally gone when Bennie insisted.

The "small adjustment" Aster's mother had made was simple. Swept up within her wings, they found themselves suddenly back at the farm, in the kitchen. A few seconds later, Darwin Basalt came staggering in, asking what on earth was going on. He'd lost three hours and couldn't explain it. Neither could Marie when she joined them. The last thing she remembered was listening to the radio while she transplanted a cactus.

No one else could explain what had happened either. No one remembered anything from the time of Aster's radio and television broadcasts, and they didn't remember those either. There was just the bizarre loss of time, for everyone in the city and nearby.

Quite a few people "woke up" with injuries, so it was easy for Bennie to say she had no clue how her arm got dislocated, and for Madir to be puzzled over the bruises on her arms, and Kim to shrug at the red mark of a burn across his chest.

He'd been worried about Chief Inspector Benison, and was relieved to see her on the seven o'clock news, which he and Eila were allowed to watch, their parents hoping that somehow the weird absence from their daily life was going to be explained. Inspector Benison was interviewed as one of the stranger cases, because most people came to themselves close to where they remembered being. But she had been in her office, and woke up to herself on the shores of the river near the lake entrance, with her pistol missing and a bruise to her head.

Many theories were presented, but nothing even close to what really happened.

"Don't throw that dart, Bennie," warned Kim. "Here, take this map."

"This is only half a map," said Bennie. "Or a quarter of one."

"That's what you found on the body of the guard at the upper gate of the pyramid," said Kim. "It is only part of a map, a map to great treasure—"

"Are we starting?" asked Theo. "I haven't decided on my last spell yet."

"And we haven't quite finished our characters," said Eila. She'd read all the rule books the day before, and Kim was already dreading the conversation about the Dungeon Master's decisions being final, regardless of what it said in the rules.

"I'm not starting," said Kim. "I'm just telling Bennie about the map."

"Well, don't," said Tamara. She took her glasses off and started to clean them. "Wait until everyone's ready."

"Okay, okay," said Kim. He settled back in his chair, wincing slightly as the electrical burn on his chest stretched.

"You know," said Bennie, "I think we should check up on something."

"What?" asked Kim.

"Aster's nest in the tower. What if it's still there? We should take a look."

Kim stared at her in horror.

"I mean, when my shoulder's better. In a couple of days—"

"It will have gone," said Eila. "Forget about it."

"The tower will be locked up again for sure, anyway," said Kim. Quickly, before Bennie could get enthusiastic about potential lockpicking, he added, "Is everyone ready now?"

"Yeah," said Theo. "I'm going with the new Strength spell from *Greyhawk*."

"Yep," confirmed Bennie.

"Uh-huh," said Tamara.

"Yes," said Eila. "Cassiopeia is ready."

"And so is Rat Thinfingers," added Madir.

"Okay," replied Kim. "Altmoor, Flàdrif, and Hargrim, you are gathered around the body of the guard inside the pyramid tunnel. Flàdrif, you've just found the map on the guard, when you hear the outer gate grind open, and two people step in from outside—"

"I ready my sword!" snapped Bennie.

"You don't have to," said Kim quicky. "You recognize

them as friends, sent to join you by the Town Wizard. A thief and a paladin. They explain that Lelanthe feared the three of you could not win through without help."

He paused, took in a deep breath and dramatically proclaimed:

"You must all work together to succeed in this quest!"

MY TEENAGE DUNGEONS & DRAGONS CAMPAIGN

I ran a campaign from the ages of thirteen to eighteen for several friends from school. During that time I developed a whole game world, and made a lot of maps, particularly for a kind of gazetteer, or guidebook, I made for the players when I was fifteen. The town of Opir, mentioned in Kim's campaign, was actually somewhere my players never visited!

TK

TK

ACKNOWLEDGMENTS

In a sense, this book began a very long time ago on a summer evening in Canberra, when I was out cycling with my friends Felicity Packard and Nicholas Cook, and we saw what we thought was a severed head in the shallow water of the lake, near where Canberra Hospital was (now the National Museum). On investigation, it turned out to be a rock and lakeweed, not a strange visitor, and we were older than the characters in this story, being sixteen or seventeen. But the seed was sown. I'd like to thank Felicity and Nick for being my friends then, now, and all the time in between.

My parents, Katharine and Henry Nix, were nothing like Kim's and Eila's parents, being open-minded; they encouraged their children in all our endeavors and interests, particularly reading whatever we wanted to read. Our house was full of books of every kind, enormously contributing to my future career as a writer. There was a period where my brothers and I did chip mortar from bricks to be used in garden paths, but we were actually paid to do so—five cents a brick! A fortune back in the 1970s to a twelve-year-old.

Speaking of my brothers, Simon and Jonathan Nix, they are also nothing like any of the characters in the book and have been wonderful siblings and friends ever since we all grew up, particularly to me. I fear that from around ages ten to eighteen, I was somewhat like Eila, except nowhere near as clever. I am still amazed my parents and brothers managed to forgive my know-it-all period.

My agents are invaluable business partners, supporters, and eternal encouragers. I am forever grateful to Jill Grinberg and her team at Jill Grinberg Literary Management in New York; Fiona Inglis and the gang at Curtis Brown Australia; and Matthew Snyder and his associates, who look after film/TV for me at CAA in Los Angeles.

My publishers are likewise essential coconspirators in this strange business of making books. A big thank you to David Levithan and the Scholastic crew in the USA; Eva Mills and everyone at Allen & Unwin in Australia; and Emma Matthewson and the team at Piccadilly Press/Bonnier in the United Kingdom. I am also very grateful to my audiobook publishers at Listening Library/Random House, and Bolinda. Similarly, I owe many thanks to my translators and the publishers who publish my books in languages other than English.

I couldn't keep on writing if it wasn't for the support of booksellers and readers everywhere. Thank you for selling books, buying books, reading books, talking about books.

Finally, once again, I would get very litte writing done without the love, support, and encouragement of my wife, Anna McFarlane, our sons, Thomas and Edward, and our dog, Snufkin.

ABOUT THE AUTHOR

Garth Nix has been a full-time writer since 2001, but has also worked as a literary agent, marketing consultant, book editor, book publicist, book sales representative, bookseller, and a part-time soldier in the Australian Army Reserve.

Garth's books include the Old Kingdom fantasy series: *Sabriel, Lirael, Abhorsen, Clariel, Goldenhand,* and *Terciel and Elinor*; science fiction novels *Shade's Children* and *A Confusion of Princes*; fantasy novels *Angel Mage, The Left-Handed Booksellers of London,* and sequel *The Sinister Booksellers of Bath*; and a Regency romance with magic, *Newt's Emerald*. His novels for children include *The Ragwitch*; the six books of the Seventh Tower sequence; *Frogkisser!,* and the Keys to the Kingdom series; plus, cowritten with Sean Williams, the TroubleTwisters and Have Sword Will Travel series.

He has written more than seventy published short

stories, some collected in *Across the Wall* and *To Hold the Bridge*, and nine stories concerning his godslaying duo are collected in *Sir Hereward and Mister Fitz: Stories of the Witch Knight and the Puppet Sorcerer*.

More than seven million copies of Garth's books have been sold around the world. They have appeared on the bestseller lists of the *New York Times*, *Publishers Weekly*, the *Bookseller*, and others, and his work has been translated into forty-two languages. He has won multiple Aurealis Awards, the ABIA Award, Ditmar Award, the Mythopoeic Award, CBCA Honour Book, and has been short-listed for the Locus Awards, the Shirley Jackson Award, and others.